I0761575

WHEN IT'S YOUR TURN FOR MIDNIGHT

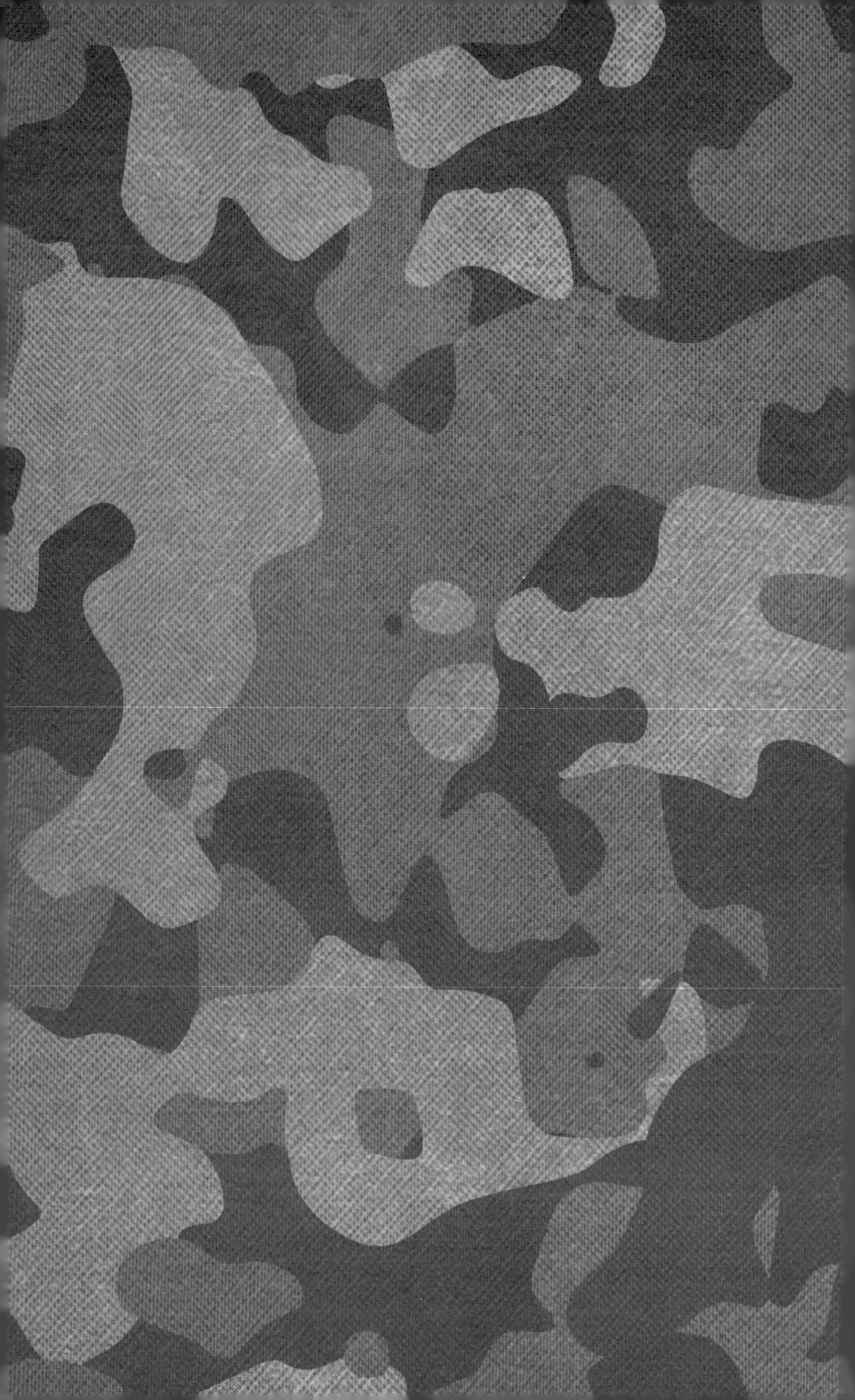

WHEN IT'S YOUR TURN FOR MIDNIGHT

Blessing Musariri

carolrhoda LAB
MINNEAPOLIS

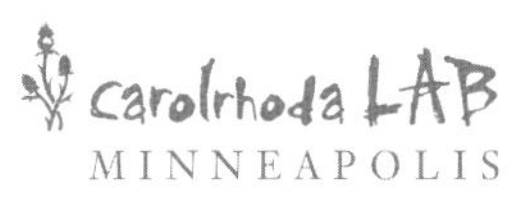

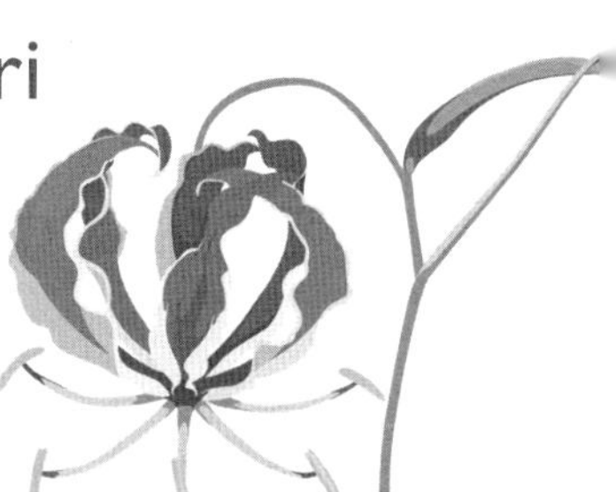

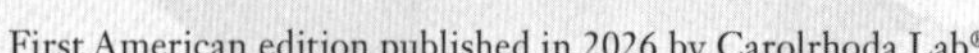
First American edition published in 2026 by Carolrhoda Lab®

First published in Great Britain in 2024 by Zephyr, and imprint of Head of Zeus, part of Bloomsbury Publishing Plc

Carolrhoda Lab®
An imprint of Lerner Publishing Group, Inc.
241 First Avenue North
Minneapolis, MN 55401 USA

For reading levels and more information, look up this title at www.lernerbooks.com.

Design elements: viktor fesyuk/Shutterstock (flowers); cornflowerz/Shutterstock (background).

Main body text set in Janson Text LT Std.
Typeface provided by Adobe Systems.

Library of Congress Cataloging-in-Publication Data

Names: Musariri, Blessing, 1973– author.
Title: When it's your turn for midnight / Blessing Musariri.
Other titles: When it is your turn for midnight
Description: First American edition. | Minneapolis : Carolrhoda Lab, 2026. | Audience term: Teenagers | Audience: Ages 13–18. | Audience: Grades 10–12. | Summary: When fifteen-year-old Chianti learns that her Baba is not her biological father, she goes to stay with her maternal grandmother, where she discovers a new definition of family.
Identifiers: LCCN 2025008902 (print) | LCCN 2025008903 (ebook) | ISBN 9798765689134 | ISBN 9798765691564 (epub)
Subjects: CYAC: Families—Fiction. | Secrets—Fiction. | Psychic trauma—Fiction. | Zimbabwe—Fiction. | LCGFT: Domestic fiction. | Novels.
Classification: LCC PZ7.1.M8934 Wh 2026 (print) | LCC PZ7.1.M8934 (ebook) | DDC [Fic]—dc23

LC record available at https://lccn.loc.gov/2025008902
LC ebook record available at https://lccn.loc.gov/2025008903

Manufactured in Guang Dong, China by Dream Colour Printing
1-1012852-54776-7/23/2025

FOR MY PARENTS

PROLOGUE

If anyone ever says to you, "Sticks and stones may break my bones, but words can never hurt me," tell them to come see me. This works on the playground when you're five and someone says your hair is like the coily thing used to scrub pots. But when it's your own mother's words that rip your life down the middle, like a page from a magazine, then you think—bones can mend. Words kill.

I don't mind that my mother named me Chianti, I mind that no one ever gets it right. People say *chee-anty* instead of *kee-anty*, so I'm known as *chee-ah* for short. It's been a losing battle since day one. I only fight it when I feel excess aggravation inside.

When I was little and I would cry, Mama used to set an alarm and say, "You have two minutes. When that alarm rings, wrap it up." There was an implied threat, but I never found out what might happen—I always followed the instruction. After that, I stopped crying altogether.

Mama once said to her mother, Ambuya Precious, "Chianti's tears are gold, Mama, extremely precious and rare. They don't come for nothing." She may have regretted training me that well, because she had a hard time figuring me out. Except for when I was angry and those unshed tears turned into words. When I'm angry my words are lava and they even burn me.

About three weeks ago, a steady stream of lava rained from my heart. A deep cavern opened and I couldn't control the hot things that escaped. After the eruption, I didn't say another word to Mama. I packed my bags and hitchhiked from Harare to Ambuya's place in Mutare.

I walked for an hour to get to her house from where I was dropped off. From past visits, I remembered the road that led from town to the avenue of red flamboyant trees at the bottom of the hill. I wasn't scared, just relieved to arrive. My tiredness had spread all the way through the inside of me to the tips of the hairs on my skin.

When she opened the front door, Ambuya didn't scold me for risking my life—after all, I could've been abducted and assaulted, could've been murdered and had my body parts used in evil magic, or could've simply disappeared to some unnamed fate. She just said, "There's no one to cook and clean up after you. Think carefully before you take another step."

I took one step, then another, dragging my bag behind me.

"Close the door after you," she said.

ONE

Mutare feels like another country. The blue shimmer in the distance fools me into believing the sea is soon after the mountains, but it's the beginning of Mozambique over there and the coastline is many miles away. Ambuya lives in a cul-de-sac at the top of a hill. Her three besties—the gogos, Stella, Tapera and Ropa—are her neighbors. Stella and Ropa are her cousins, and Tapera is a friend they met when they were all fighting in the war to liberate Zimbabwe from colonial powers, long before I was born.

It's quiet here. In Harare, we live in a gated complex, but once you leave, it's loud and bustling. Mutare is more chill, even the busy parts; there aren't enough people to make it hectic. Ambuya and the gogos have extensive yards, almost a world unto themselves. Standing on the balcony of my room, I watch the sun rise over the treetops and crest the mountain. I imagine I'm on a vacation and never have to leave.

I thought Ambuya would come to wake me, the way Sisi Taku does at home, but there's no knock at my door, no smell of oats, no sounds of Taren and Tisha. One morning I took a picture of my sisters lurching about like sleepy orangutans, and they laughed and laughed and laughed.

That day, Tisha's hair was sticking up every whichway because she'd refused to have it plaited. Tisha is nine, and tender-headed to the end of all days. You only have to hold a comb and she will have anxiety. When I'm in a good mood I'll do her hair, and she doesn't fight me. She says I'm gentle. Taren, on the other hand, is a total diva—she scowls and fidgets, gives incessant directions, keeps reaching up to feel how it's going, and holds a mirror to her face every five seconds. She's thirteen going on twenty-five, and Mama says I'm going on fifty.

I go from room to room, standing in the doorway of each one, my thoughts refusing to stay still long enough for me to settle them. I open doors, close them, remembering nothing I've seen.

Not much interests me until the last room, at the end of the house. There's a mishmash of things in boxes, on shelves, in suitcases, as if Ambuya got fed up of unpacking when she moved in and just shoved everything in here. At my feet is a medium-sized cardboard box with loose photos, papers, notebooks, and albums. The picture on top is of a young girl in a school uniform. I'm pretty sure it's Mama because the girl looks like Tisha.

I flick through photos, taking guesses at who's who. Several have names and dates written on the backs. I can usually pick out the gogos. They're mostly together, in a photo studio or out and about—war and peace, I think as I flip through a bunch from their fighting days.

One photo in particular catches and holds my attention. Piercing eyes shine through black face paint while she balances a rocket launcher on her shoulders. I know it isn't Ambuya, but I can't figure out which of the gogos it is. She looks like nothing could take her down and the world had better beware. I need that kind of attitude myself—the kind that conveys fearlessness without my having to say a single word.

In a corner of the room is a pile of empty shoeboxes. One thing about Ambuya is she loves shoes; her dressing room has shelves and shelves of them. Tisha, Taren, and I had a blast in there once, trying on her stuff.

On a shelf above the boxes are school art supplies, probably destined for preschools as a donation: colored pens and pencils, glitter, paints, brushes. I select a few things and, as I make my way out, grab a couple of shoe boxes—the cardboard will make good canvases.

Despite what she said, Ambuya has put food on the table consistently since I've been here. She's otherwise left me alone and it's been a blessing. She goes in and out of the house; I hear her car start up several times a day. But today is different. When I walk into the sunny kitchen, Ambuya is sitting at the table peering over her rhinestone glasses at a tablet in her hands. There's a cup of tea next to her, plus a plate of peeled, boiled sweet potatoes and samosas. I'm no longer surprised at my grandmother's strange food combinations.

"Ahh, you're awake. Good morning, Queen Elizabeth," she says. My grace period is over.

"Good morning, Ambuya," I say, "how did you sleep?"

"I slept well if you slept well."

Duly I reply, "I slept well."

From the moment I stopped talking to Mama, I've been in the deep end of weariness. I feel as if I die at night and resurrect in the morning. I don't even dream.

I haven't told Ambuya why I came, but she'll have an idea that it's trouble with Mama. They are not the best of friends, and Mama won't come looking for me here. Taren would've told her where I was going. She's no snitch, but she's not about other people's problems either; she's got enough of her own.

Ambuya indicates the place setting near her chair. I sit down and pull the teapot toward me. It's milky rooibos, brewed the way I like it. I reach for a samosa, and Ambuya makes a steeple for her chin with her fingers and watches me chew.

She's nothing like what a grandmother called Ambuya should look like. She's wearing sporty chartreuse sweats and has a multi-colored hairband around a light brown twist-out style. She's tall and fit and looks like she could go a few rounds in a boxing ring.

"I guess you'd better tell me what happened. Taren has been flooding my phone with texts, but none of them say anything useful."

I'm not ready to jump into the story yet. I have to fetch it from the recent archives in my brain and there's no intern to send. I don't want to go myself. "Did you know?" I ask.

"Know what, my dear?" Ambuya used to be an ambassador, so she always hedges her bets.

"You know what I'm talking about."

"How could I possibly know? I understand this has to do with your mother, but it could be any number of things."

"And Tinashe." I use his given name instead of calling him Baba.

At this, she raises one heavily filled-in eyebrow. "Tinashe?"

"Yes, Tinashe," I reply.

She lifts her teacup and takes a sip, cuts a disc of sweet potato in half and pops it in her mouth. "You'd better just tell me."

We shouldn't have joked.

We were sitting at the dining table doing our homework. It had been a rough few days. Mama and Baba had been getting into it all week. I used to wonder what they even liked about each other. Mama is a singer and Baba is a financial something or other—and she is too much for him to handle.

Mama had come home late from a gig, and the next day, Baba did the same. Mama lost her cool and threw stuff. The night before had been quite wild. I was looking at a mark on the corner of the table, where a flying pot had chipped the wood, and said, "God must have been too lazy to do his homework when he put Mama and Baba together, because eesh!"

Taren laughed. "Tell me about it! How did they even make us? They're like a snot-shooting sneeze and a poopy fart all at once—bad combination."

It took me a minute to picture it and when I did, I laughed and laughed until I farted by mistake, and then Taren and Tisha laughed until one drooled over her book and the other fell off her chair. Taren can be rude, but she's also funny, which means trouble.

In my mind, that joke marked a shift in our cosmos that made our lives change gear.

"It was just a joke," Ambuya said, wiping tears from her cheeks. "You kids are funny, but completely out of order. Don't tell me *that's* what got everyone in such a fury."

I sigh from the depths of my soul, and tears prick the corners of my eyes. I don't want to cry. I blink them away.

"No," I say, "that came a few days later."

Mama is never, ever, *ever* on time and it drives us up the wall. I've been campaigning for a car for my sixteenth birthday—I'll be able to get my license then. We're so traumatized by

Mama's chronic lateness that I don't even care if it's not a cool car, as long as it works. We all need this.

It's stressful to always be running to class in the morning. It ruins your whole day. We arrive when the roll's been called and homework's been handed in. We get manual labor and have to pick up litter during break. Why do they punish us? It's not our fault. They should punish Mama.

"Why don't you go to school with your father?"

"We'd have to leave at five-thirty in the morning when he goes to the gym, and we'd be too early."

"Hmmm" is all Ambuya says.

We were imagining being in a car, going where we needed to. Mama and Baba were in the house. So we decided to actually get inside Mama's car. We liked to sit in there so we wouldn't hear them shouting. We'd play music and pretend that we were on a road trip. That we were far away.

I sat behind the wheel. Taren and Tisha settled in, one in the passenger seat, the other behind me. I adjusted the seat and the mirror and turned the key in the ignition for the radio to come on. But I turned it too far and the car shot forward.

We went into Baba's Range Rover with a tremendous jolt and a sickening crunch. Mouths open, we stared at each other before Tisha squealed and scrambled out. Me and Taren, we panicked and did the same, dashing to the edge of the yard. We hid behind the peach tree and the rose bushes, shaking like tambourines at a hippie festival.

Mama and Baba came out to see what the hullaballoo was about. They walked around the cars, Baba running an agitated hand over his head. He looked in our direction, as if he could see through the leaves and branches, and shouted, "Taren!"

Tisha's arms were around my neck like a garrote as she scrambled up my back, her skinny knees digging into my ribs. Next to us, Taren was shaking herself into death. She was breathing like she'd run ten miles. Then her eyes rolled up and she passed out. I didn't blame her—she was already on her last warning for her firefighting stint in the laundry room the week before. They should've just named her Trouble and quit being surprised by her antics.

I felt like fainting too, but I stood, Tisha still on me, and said, "Taren's passed out, Baba! We need a doctor!"

Ridiculous, yes. What else could I say? I wanted to cry, but what would have been the use?

If I never talk about what came next, maybe things can return to the way they were. Maybe we can forget about it. After almost sixteen years, how can one short sentence cause such devastation?

TWO

The sun shining on the table makes me wonder what the time is. I haven't had my phone on much since I arrived. Taren keeps texting, asking if I'm mad at her. She doesn't get it, that I don't want to talk. There's too much going on.

Ambuya doesn't say things just to say them. If she's got nothing of any use to you, she keeps her peace and gets on with her life. I can deal with this.

"So! You have the accident with the car, Taren passes out, you're in big trouble. I know your parents—what was the punishment?"

"That's the thing," I say. "What happened was worse than any punishment."

Ambuya sips her tea.

I finally have to give words to it. I need to search for them, put them in order, test them. I clear my throat because there's a roadblock. Checkpoints are necessary—words are dangerous things, they cannot be let out at will.

"Um . . ." I clear my throat again. "Uh . . . umm . . ."

Taren didn't pass out for long. By the time Mama reached us, she was coming round. Baba stayed where he was, fuming.

"It wasn't Taren," I said, "and it was an accident. I didn't mean to do it."

None of us had ever seen Baba that mad, and it was actually frightening. He grabbed my arm and dragged me to the cars.

"Look what you did! Do you have any idea what could've happened? You might've hurt yourselves!"

I remember thinking he probably wasn't as worried about that as he was about his precious, expensive car. He was still holding my arm in a death grip.

"You leave her alone!" Mama shouted. "Don't touch her, she's not your child!"

Everything stopped in that moment. Baba let me go like I was a hot thing off the stove.

The silence should've ended the world. I was suspended in a bubble without understanding, only knowing that what I'd heard was the sound of something irreparable breaking.

"Oh, Tamara!" Ambuya sits back with her hand across her mouth and shakes her head.

My tea has gone cold. I take a sip, though it's as if nothing can get past my throat.

"He said, 'What did you say?' And she stood there, like she was telling him we were driving to the shops: 'She's not your child, don't touch her.' Ambuya, even in hell they don't know the true meaning of *All hell broke loose*. Or maybe they're used to it down there, so it's not as shocking as when it happens in your own yard. Usually it's Mama who's out of control, but this time it was him—should I still call him Baba?"

I wait for Ambuya to give me guidance, but she says nothing. The sun cutting a strip across her face brings my attention to her eyes, which are hazel like mine. We have the same birthmark on the inside of our left elbow too. At least it's definite that she's my grandmother.

I don't notice that the silence has stretched until Ambuya prompts me. "What happened next?"

He dived for Mama and they started screaming at each other. Tisha grabbed Baba's leg and Taren was trying to pull him away. Then Mukoma Ben came running. He'd been watering the vegetables—he was still holding the hose. He started spraying everyone, saying, "Hey! Hey! Hey!"

Sisi came running out of the house and stood there with her hands around her head, saying, "Maiwee, maiwee kani, don't kill her, boss! Please!" Then she tried to grab Tisha but got caught in the crossfire. I'm not sure if one of my parents pushed her away or if she just lost her footing, but she fell—her body dropped and took the rest of them along. They all tumbled to the ground.

I was a statue. I stood there watching and then I began to laugh. I was in pain from laughing. Tears were leaking from my eyes and I fell against the wall holding my stomach. Then I choked on spit and coughed until I vomited. It was a mess.

We sit in silence. The sounds outside drift in through the windows: an insect buzzing, birds twittering, sprinklers, a dog barking, and the faraway noise of cars on the main road. The words I've gathered together are finished. I feel as if I've been sitting with Ambuya for half a life, narrating an absurd vaudevillian production.

Finally, Ambuya sighs, gets up from her chair, places her hands around my face, and kisses me. Her scent lingers—fresh and light.

"Come," she says, "we've got work to do."

THREE

After the tea we walk across to Gogo Stella's house. She's not actually my grandmother—none of them are except for Ambuya and that's why I call only her Ambuya, even though *gogo* and *ambuya* mean the same thing. They're all grandmothers.

"Chianti!" Gogo Stella engulfs me in a soft, heavily perfumed hug. "Look at you!" She holds me at arm's length and beams through her ruby lipstick. "You've come to visit your gogos. How lovely. Lucky us. Come in, come in."

Gogo Stella's house is an emporium of fabulousness, busy and colorful to the extent that if you're not in the right frame of mind you feel dizzy and disoriented. Her garden, too, is a profusion of riotous color, scents, and movement, as if the birds and insects are on stimulants. The nature is loud and in your face.

She leads us into a garage that's more like a wide-open studio, piled high with clothes and shoes and handbags. The floor is tiled and clean, and the walls are shelved with baskets. On the floor along one wall are large bins of clothes, and more clothes are on a rack in the rear of the room.

I see now why Ambuya has given me time to recover from my trip. The energy of the people in this room would've been enough to knock me out a few days ago. I'm hugged and petted and admired to Harare and beyond.

"Here is a young person to worry about your Flip Flop videos, Mr. Kingsley Pfupajena," Gogo Tapera announces, presenting me as if I'm a prize.

"TikTok," corrects Mr. Kingsley Pfupajena, a dapper old man in a coral jacket, white pants, and a navy striped tie. He's been filming something on his phone but sets it down now. "Hello, Miss Chianti Minana."

He says my name correctly, so I smile. "Hello. What should I call you?"

"Call me Mr. Kingsley Pfupajena! I'm not a shortcut, my dear. I have a name for a reason, and that is to give it life. Every occasion my full name is called, I am obliged to step up and live the full life of that name."

"He handles Chedu's social media," Ambuya explains, using the name of the gogos' fashion brand.

Gogo Stella says dryly, "Because he's so in tune with the youth."

"I may not be as young as I used to be," says Mr. Kingsley Pfupajena, "and it's true I never had children of my own, but I helped raise plenty—including your mother," he adds, looking at me. Sizing me up, he asks, "Can you dance?"

"Um . . . it depends."

"I'm okay with that," he responds with a gleeful smile. "The only unacceptable answer would've been no."

"Leave her alone, she's not here to be exploited," Ambuya says. "Sit over there, Chianti, next to Tapera."

"Hello, Gogo," I say as I squeeze onto the weathered leather sofa.

"Sit, sit, muzukuru," she says, moving a pile of yellow things. "We're sorting through the merchandise."

Ambuya sits at a table and opens a large notebook. Across from her, Gogo Stella picks up a pile of papers and begins going through them. Gogo Ropa, more subdued than the others, is working through a heap of men's pants.

Of the gogos, she's the most surprising. She wears a nose ring, sports bright eye shadow over dramatic eyeliner that I'm not sure is intentional, and has very short hair. She has on a khaki shirt and pants that look like a uniform and lace-up boots, as if she were in the army. She doesn't talk much, just methodically picks out clothes and puts them in another pile.

Gogo Tapera and Gogo Stella have lively faces and bright smiles. Both are wearing tie-dye boubous. Gogo Stella's hair is piled high on her head—extensions of some sort—and Gogo Tapera's salt-and-pepper locs are loose.

"What are you doing with all of this?" I ask Gogo Tapera.

"Well, we go to the salaula market in town and buy various items from secondhand clothing bales. Then we put them together and decide what to do with them. You can get brand-new stuff, like this"—she holds up a yellow shirt with a shop tag on it—"and sometimes you get designer shoes and handbags that need a little brushing up. We pay small money and make them more interesting by adding our own designs and whatnot. And then no two things are exactly alike." Gogo Tapera laughs as if the thought of that end result completely sparks her life. "When we've made the clothes new again, we sell them online."

"Are you allowed to do that?" I ask.

"We're doing it, so there! What are you—the fashion police?"

Ambuya laughed. "I told you, Stella. These born-frees are clueless about life. Do you think we put in an application to the Smith regime to start a war? No one gave us permission for anything. We took it by force."

Inwardly, I roll my eyes. This is what I get for running away to stay with ex-combatants.

Gogo Tapera continues. "My daughter in Washington handles our distribution overseas—your auntie Dorothy. She grew up with your mom."

I don't want to think about Mama just now, so I ask quickly, "Where do the clothes bales come from?"

"Well, that's a good question for two reasons," says Mr. Kingsley Pfupajena. Gogo Ropa, I notice, seems to be in a world of her own, continuing to pick up clothes from one pile and put them in another.

Mr. Kingsley Pfupajena explains, "The vendors at the salaula market buy bales of goods, sight unseen, from people who advertise them for sale from Mozambique . . ."

"And who might those people be?" Gogo Stella asks.

"I'll get to that," Mr. Kingsley Pfupajena says testily.

"Uh-huh. You should do more market runs with us instead of spending all your time on your Tok Tok, day in, day out."

Mr. Kingsley Pfupajena doesn't bother to correct her, just rolls his eyes and continues, "Anyway! It's kind of a lottery. The more you pay, the better stuff you get in the bale."

"That's why we have certain vendors we work with," interrupts Gogo Tapera. "They call us first if they have quality pieces, especially designer brands. We've always loved fashion, and we're handy and creative so . . ."

When they first started up, she explains, they were just doing it for themselves, but they enjoyed it so much and received so many compliments that they soon turned to orders. Auntie Dorothy got most of their first sales through her friends, and social media did the rest.

"It's all well and good making the stuff, but I'm the marketing mastermind," says Mr. Kingsley Pfupajena.

Gogo Stella's response to that is a grunt, and she rips a shirt apart at the seams with a little too much force.

"Before we get into this 'who's more important to the operation' fight again," Ambuya says, "let's focus on the problem at hand."

I have to really pay attention because they all start talking at once—except for Gogo Ropa, who doesn't stop her rhythmic sorting of clothes.

In the end I understand that the government has banned the importing of secondhand clothes to protect the textile manufacturers. But with the economy being bad, few people can afford to buy new things . . . They talk about smuggling and undesignated crossing points, which are sort of interesting, but I keep being drawn to Gogo Ropa picking up and putting down, and wrestling a thread in my mind that's trying to escape me.

It's only when she stops and looks right at me that I figure out what it is—the eyes! Rocket-launcher Gogo from the photo I found!

I suddenly feel nervous and look away.

Mr. Kingsley Pfupajena has decided we're best friends and age-mates despite his shock of white hair. He won't stop talking to me about TikTok and a YouTuber he follows. Gogo Tapera is talking about robbers intercepting the smugglers who bring in the bales of goods, and Gogo Stella and Ambuya are arguing loudly about politics.

In the middle of this, I realize Gogo Ropa has disappeared. None of us heard or saw her leave. I understand why she decided to go and I want to slip away too. There's far too much verve and crackle from people who should really not have these levels of energy.

I've met all the gogos before, but I've never really thought of their everyday lives. They've always been background props, adding color and dimension here and there. Now in their world, I am the prop. The granddaughter. It feels strange, as if I have to find a way to latch on and be real. And that won't be easy—the apocalyptic wasteland of my life won't let me lose sight of what brought me here.

I finally tell Ambuya that I'd like to go home. I expect

her to give me chores to do but she simply says, "Okay, see you later."

Back home in Harare, everything is an instruction or an order. Mama is good at these if nothing else. I've always been her remote control by which she gets things done. She doesn't spend a lot of actual time at home. Even now she's on tour in Europe with her band—like she didn't just explode a land mine in her own backyard and leave a gaping hole where her family should be.

FOUR

I drift through the rooms of Ambuya's house. There are photos on all the walls—most of them of her years as a diplomat, posing with dignitaries and other people from that part of her life. I recognize Hugh Masekela, the South African jazz musician. A young Mama is in that picture, and she's told us the story of how they met in New York when apartheid was still the law in South Africa. She has the same photo at home.

I'm not angry with her anymore. I don't know how I feel. I'm numb.

When the situation calmed down—wet people dried and changed, vomit cleaned up and tempers dimmed—we were in a daze. Baba got in his car and drove off. Mama shut herself in her room. I felt shaky and empty inside, like if someone had dropped a marble in my mouth it would've made a racket rolling around.

"Mama," I said. I didn't knock, just opened the door and walked in. She was sitting on the bench at the end of the bed, staring at nothing. "Mama, why would you say that?" My voice sounded as if it were coming from a place that wasn't my body.

She didn't respond.

"Mama!" I spoke more loudly, and my voice caught so that I had to start again. "Tell me why you said what you said."

Finally she looked at me and said, "Because it's true."

"What do you *mean* it's true?"

"It's true, Tinashe is not your biological father. I was pregnant by another man when I decided to marry him, and there was never any need to say anything about it."

Just like that. As if I were her friend that she was playing Truth or Dare with and she had chosen "truth." I understood then why Tinashe had lunged at her.

"So you were a two-timing party girl who slept around and decided to stick to a fool with money who didn't have the good sense to see what you were?"

"Don't you talk to me like that!"

"Don't you sit there and tell me Tinashe is not my father like it doesn't matter!" I shouted. And then I couldn't stop shouting. "It matters, it matters to me. It changes everything. Who are *you*? Are you my mother or did you lie about that too? You hate Tinashe more than you love us—do you realize that?"

I was now screaming.

"You're horrible, you're horrible and I hate you! You didn't care that you were breaking our hearts and killing our family. You're an assassin. That's what you are!" I was vibrating. Words came out on their own.

When I was finally quiet, I felt lightheaded and couldn't move. I was afraid I might disintegrate into a heap on the floor if I tried.

Mama got up, walked to the en suite bathroom, closed the door and locked it.

I don't know how long I stood there. I don't remember how I got to bed. I don't remember anything until I woke up the next day to find that Tisha and Taren had been packed up and taken to Ambuya Minana—Tinashe's mother—no longer my grandmother, I guess. Blood speaks.

Tinashe had also packed up and gone. It was just me and Mama, and soon Mama wasn't even there either.

My room is neat and full of shadows from the trees outside. I haven't unpacked my bag. Toiletries spill out on the small white dressing table. Sitting on the bed, I arrange my supplies. I cut open one side of a shoebox. It's gray and black on the outside—perfect, I think as I start to draw.

Before she met and married Tinashe, Mama had a tiger tattooed on her thigh. She smoked cigarettes and drank beer straight from the bottle. Her clothes, which she sewed herself, always looked like they'd run out of fabric. They were short, tight, and full of gaps. She spent a lot of time in clubs, where she performed. That's how she met Tinashe, at his company Christmas party when he was a trainee manager. He had a midi afro and thick glasses and dressed like he was ten, going to Sunday church. Shame, he was no match for Mama.

After their wedding, the gaps in Mama's clothes started to disappear and her costumes became more about art. Even her music became original—a kind of Afro-pop, mixing traditional with contemporary. When I think of her I feel myself burning up, and breathing becomes impossible.

I switch on my phone to check the clock. Thirty-six messages from Taren pop up. The last one says, ***Lucky you staying with Ambuya Precious, this one is the worst***, then lots of emojis. I wonder how Tisha is doing—Ambuya Minana makes Tisha mute.

Not my problem, I tell myself. Not my grandmother, only half my sisters. But it's my angry brain saying that. My heart is worried.

I switch off the phone. There were no messages from Mama and anyway I wouldn't have opened them. I hoped Baba would've sent me a message, but there's nothing.

The light has gone. I've been busy with my shoebox and my thoughts. Ambuya isn't here, and if they mean to get through all the piles of clothes they had in front of them, she won't be back for a while.

I put my shoebox on the floor. I've drawn a woman with a tiger tattoo behind bars. She has red lips and is holding a smoking cigarette in her hands. She doesn't care about anything.

I open the other side of the shoebox and paint a blue sky with clouds and birds. The sun is shining.

The woman is alone in her cell. She doesn't need anybody; next to her, she has her guitar, and any time she feels lonely, she can sing herself a song.

FIVE

It's not yet light when Ambuya leaves the house, but I'm awake. She told me that she would be up early for the secondhand clothes market and that I was not to worry when I heard her leave. She's given me keys to the house. I've never had keys to a house before. At home there's always someone around—if it's not Sisi Taku, it's Mukoma Ben, and while the doors are usually unlocked, going past the gate without permission is another matter.

It doesn't feel strange to be in Ambuya's house alone—no one would dare come in with ill intentions.

My second shoebox now shows an image of Ambuya and the gogos in the bush. They're wearing designer gear and holding guns and war manifestos—I've cut out their figures from one of the photos that had a duplicate. It didn't have Mr. Kingsley Pfupajena in it, so I've drawn him in. In my picture he's sitting on a rock taking a photo of the gogos. I cut out leaves from bits of fabric and make flowers from paper.

I pick up the photo of Gogo Ropa, the one with the rocket launcher. She is focused, so sure of what she's carrying on her shoulders that it makes perfect sense how she survived. When I think of Ambuya and the other gogos during the war, I picture them having a blast—no pun intended. It's an absurd thought, but it's hard to imagine anything else.

When I have breakfast, it's bright and hot and Ambuya is still at large. I make my way outside via the wooden front door. Carefully I lock it behind me, pocketing my keys.

Ambuya has a big lawn and trimmed bushes, beautiful tall rose bushes in full bloom, and behind the house a whole forest of trees. It looks like you could walk in and find a different country on the other side. I imagine a humongous python coming out of the forest, sliding through my window to hide under my bed and strangle me in my sleep. I put a hand to my throat, starting, as if the thing has actually happened. Breathlessly, I consider going back in and shutting the windows.

At the gate, I hesitate. I'm completely exposed. I think of the baby chicks that hawks scoop up for dinner. Is there a bird buff enough to carry me away?

The cul-de-sac is quiet-quiet. I wonder if I'm in a real place—what if it's all been a dream and I'm going to wake up and find that nothing has changed? That we're still together and no one has said the words from hell? Someone should wake me because I'm failing to do it myself.

Gogo Stella's gate is locked from the outside—they're still out. I walk aimlessly, following the curve of the street.

Mr. Kingsley Pfupajena also lives in this cul-de-sac. Maybe he didn't go to the market?

As I reach the midpoint of the cul-de-sac, I see a brown gate that's slightly open. I guess this is Gogo Ropa's house. It has the mood of her in her utilitarian khaki outfit. The house blends into the emptiness, almost as if it's a mirage.

I peep in, and I'm surprised to see a wide expanse of paving, broken only by succulents. It's like the wasteland scene of my life has become a reality. It's not apocalyptic, but it's right for Gogo Ropa. I'm almost expecting the flash and boom of detonation, but there's just silence.

From a guava tree near the gate, a bright orange bird trills a song as if it's announcing me. I push the gate, which makes a loud groaning sound, and walk cautiously forward.

"Gogogoyi!" I call out as I reach the door. Announcing yourself like that has nothing to do with the word for *grandmother*; it mimics the sound of knocking—*gho gho gho!* Strangely it doesn't occur to me to actually knock. I'm not certain why I'm here, but here I am.

"Gogo Ropa," I say. "It's me, Chianti."

There's a flicker at one of the windows, and I hear footsteps.

Gogo Ropa opens the door and looks at me. She's dressed much the same as yesterday, complete with bright eye shadow. She doesn't say anything, just walks back into the house. I guess that's what they do with visitors here—giving them one last chance to leave.

I close the door and follow her into a spacious room where the curtains are drawn almost all the way shut. Gogo

Ropa is already seated in an armchair near the windows. I go in and sit on the sofa.

On a side table next to her is a glass. She lifts it up and takes a sip, then holds it out to me. "Whisky?"

"Um." I clear my throat. "I'm fifteen, Gogo. I don't drink."

She takes another sip. "You don't drink." She says this with finality, as if making a mental note.

There's a shaft of light coming through the gap in the curtains, and dust motes float in the air.

"It's a different time," she says. "Fifteen these days is still a child, is it?"

"Yes," I say.

"And you still feel like one?"

"Yes," I say. "Although *whose* child is another thing."

"It matters," she says, "whose child you are?"

I stop to think about this. "I guess I want to be someone's child. I'm currently only half in the family equation. The other half is unaccounted for." My throat tightens up. "Gogo, may I get a glass of water?"

"Glasses are in the cupboard above the sink. Our tap water is good here."

I get up and walk toward the kitchen. I notice the walls are chockablock with framed photos and artwork of rural scenes. I don't linger but go directly to the cluttered kitchen and pour myself a glass. I take it with me back to the lounge.

"I ran away to war when I was seventeen," she starts without preamble. "My father was ready to marry me off to pay a debt. I told my mother I would rather die. And so when the boys in the bush came round and compelled us to attend a pungwe—we sang and danced all night and listened to political teachings and war manifestos—I never returned home. See these?"

She pushes up her sleeves to reveal scarred elbows.

"These are my badges of freedom. In training we crawled for hours, over rocks and scrub and sand, hands and knees. Training to move undetected in the bush. Life or death. Others complained the pain was unbearable. Overnight the cuts and scrapes would start to heal, and the next day we broke them open again. The pain meant freedom to me, even before the war was won."

I can't relate to what Gogo Ropa is saying. It's almost a folktale—nothing in the region of my life problems. I think of Taren, who acts like she's Dr. Phil. I hear her voice saying, *Are you invalidating my experience just because yours was different?*

"They're just scars now," Gogo Ropa continues. "I don't remember the pain, only the story of it. Much more came after, and with each event, things changed. Like when you're driving a car, the gear shifts, different actions take place in the engine, but you're still moving. Whether forward or backward, or left or right, is your choice." She sips her whisky. "Why did you come here?"

"I was looking for Ambuya Precious, but she's at the market with the other gogos," I say. Simpler.

"Those ones!" she shakes her head. "They don't listen. Too much chattering."

That's Taren and Tisha. I get it.

Taking stock of the room, I notice a computer on the dining room table, one of the old PCs. The monitor shows different views of the yard. "You have CCTV, Gogo?"

"No one can sneak up on me. It makes better sense than a garden full of trees and noise from birds and creatures. How would you notice an intruder lurking?"

"The war is over," I say, envisioning both Ambuya's and Gogo Stella's yards, the lushness and the colors of them.

"Wars never end, my dear, they just change location."

This is true, I guess. We have a war at home and I ran away from it. People survive—this is obvious. Gogo Ropa has scars. I'm sure the other gogos and Mr. Kingsley Pfupajena have not forgotten. I wonder what it was like for them, the parts that were hard. When they went hungry, when they were cold and afraid, or if they saw their friends die.

If Mama died on tour, what would I do? What would Tinashe do? He would leave Taren and Tisha at Ambuya Minana's and forget about me. I would have to live here. But what if Ambuya didn't want the responsibility of me? What about school?

My chest is screwing itself into a tight ball, squeezing my breath, until a sharp sound intervenes. After a second or two I recognize Ambuya's car horn. They're home.

My hand is twisted in my shirt. I'm sweating and breathless. Gogo Ropa is watching me calmly. She sips her whisky and puts it down.

"You're not dying," she says. "No one ever really wants to die, even when they think they do. You don't stop breathing and then die; you die first. But if you don't stop breathing, you have to carry on. You have to carry on."

I'm not certain what she means, but I sense that she's dismissing me. It's not a bullet wound, but it's something. It hurts. I don't know what I was searching for, but I haven't found it. In fact, I feel worse. Maybe the way she's different from the other gogos made me believe we were kindred.

"I'll come back, Gogo, Ambuya is home," I say. I take my glass to the kitchen and despite the mess in there, I wash it and put it neatly away.

SIX

It's late morning and Ambuya has brought me back to Gogo Stella's garage-turned-workroom, which seems to be Command Central. Gogo Ropa isn't there and neither is Mr. Kingsley Pfupajena. Gogos Stella and Tapera are discussing repairs and upcycling ideas around a wooden table cluttered with sewing, and Ambuya is doing an inventory on her computer.

Ambuya has put me to work uploading photos of new merchandise. "I'll go in and price it later."

I sit and work across the table from her on Mr. Kingsley Pfupajena's laptop. "You're old fogies but you're really with it," I say.

Ambuya gives me a look over her glasses that says *watch it*, but Gogo Tapera and Gogo Stella hoot with laughter.

"Lofty praise from the small girl!" Gogo Tapera says. "Stick around and we'll show you a thing or two. We haven't been around the block just to be around the block, sweetheart. I wouldn't be fifteen again if you paid me a million dollars."

"Because you'd have to do all of it over," Ambuya says with talking eyes. They fall silent for a minute and I know they're remembering when they left their homes to fight in the war.

"Still," says Gogo Tapera brightly, "it's come to this." She holds up a taupe designer jacket. It now has detailed embroidery of birds on the lapels and pockets in gold and shimmering green thread. The stylized label of Chedu is on the inside pocket.

Many of the pieces Mama wears onstage have that label on them. "Mama gets a lot of stuff from you," I say.

"She does," Ambuya replies.

"I thought you two didn't get along."

"Getting along has nothing to do with anything," Gogo Stella says. "Tamara understands where she comes from. She's always been like that—we don't pay attention to her ways. She's our daughter and that's that."

This statement makes me curious, especially considering my altered situation. The gogos all claim Mama as their daughter, since they helped Ambuya bring her up. Mama lived with each of them at some point. There are dozens of photos of her in Ambuya Stella's house, as if she's her child, and I'm sure she's in Gogo Tapera's house as well. I don't remember seeing any in Gogo Ropa's, but there were so many I could've missed them.

Not much is ever said about Mama's father, and I've never thought of Ambuya as having a husband. I want to know why. I wonder if any of he's in any of the old photos. I make a mental note to investigate further.

"What happened to Sekuru, Mama's dad?" I say.

It's like I've started a game of Statue. All the gogos freeze briefly before resuming movement—a glitch in the Matrix. My new understanding of family means new thoughts, new questions. Funny how one change affects everything, like a tremor, bringing diamonds to the surface of the earth, or oil, or skeletons . . .

"More important," says Gogo Tapera, "I've run out of the white shirts I need to complete the line I'm working on. My supplier has lost two consignments to those bloody thugs. She's the only one who gives me anything of workable quality."

"True," Gogo Stella replies. "But we can't go to the police with this issue. We have to solve the problem ourselves."

I blink, do a double take. What just happened? Am I even here?

"Ambuya," I say, "I asked a question about Sekuru."

"Sure, dear, but we have a serious problem. Stella, I'm seeing we've been out of stock of blazers for a while and they're our bestsellers."

"I'm not getting good enough quality from the other vendors. We've also had no handbags for a while, and they bring in the most money for the least amount of stock."

"We need to take action," Ambuya said. "Kiki, any ideas?"

I shake my head and decide I've had enough of them. They're deliberately ignoring my question, just like Gogo

Ropa watched me fall apart without reacting. These old ladies only care about themselves and their clothes and their silly secrets. No wonder Ambuya and Mama don't get along.

But by the time I've walked through Gogo Stella's raucous, riotous garden, I'm not cross anymore and I wonder what Gogo Ropa is doing shut up in her house.

In the two weeks before I came to Ambuya's, I was always late for school. But for once, I didn't care. It meant I didn't have to see Tisha and Taren. I didn't want to see them, didn't want to discuss the issue ad nauseam. Didn't. Want. To. Talk.

Since I've been at Ambuya's, I've realized I was ashamed. As if something bad about me had been put in the spotlight for everyone to see, and Taren and Tisha held that ugly thing in their hearts and in their eyes. I was glad when Mama went on tour. I was glad when school ended. I was glad when I left home.

One of the afternoons before I left, Baba's tete, his aunt, came to see us. She brought along Tete Tabitha—Baba's sister, our aunt—and Babamunini Tatenda, Baba's younger brother. Big Tete, Little Tete, and Junior Dad. It was a delegation.

Mama didn't bother to call her people; she just asked her backup singer and best friend, Celia, to be there. She didn't say much when Big Tete asked her if it was true. She simply said, "Yes," and stared out of the window.

Little Tete said, "Mai Chia, we aren't here to judge you. We're here to help. Tinashe, understandably, is upset, but if you're both willing, we can try and fix things. Think about your girls . . ."

Mama acted like she wasn't there, even taking out her phone to check her messages. Finally, she looked up and said, "Thank you, Tete. I appreciate your coming to see me, but I have a flight to catch."

Babamunini Tatenda coaxed Mama into walking in the yard with him—they've always been good friends. To tell the truth, if you can't be friends with Babamunini Tatenda there is something seriously the matter with you. He's nice, really nice. I didn't hear what they said, but in the living room, Little Tete said, "Eesh! Mai Chia is hard work!"

Big Tete shushed her and said, "People are different."

I wanted to step out from behind the wall and say, "What about me? Does anyone care what I feel?" I guess they were more concerned with trying to reconcile the family. But even I didn't know what Mama wanted. I was afraid she'd said nothing because she had nothing left to say and it was over. Finito! When Mama is done, she is done. I was holding on to the last flimsy hope that maybe she was waiting for Baba to forgive her, that they'd get back together and work it out.

He's the only father I have. I don't want another family. I don't want another dad. But do you really get a choice with family? Seems to me you get what you get and you have to make it work.

Why doesn't he call me? Even Mama has called, but I don't pick up. I don't reply to her texts either—she doesn't say much anyway, just sends emojis, like we're pals. When I first got a phone at age twelve, I used to send her emoji stories and she'd respond like that and we made it a fun game. I'm not doing that now. There's nothing fun about this and it's definitely no game. She needs to sit in a corner and think about what she did. Only she's not thinking, she's singing.

It's late afternoon and I'm back in the room with all the things. I like it in here; it's like a cool cave. After my visit to Gogo Ropa's, I'm curious about the war. What it must've been like. Ambuya and the gogos are living as if they have no scars. I believed that was true, until I saw Gogo Ropa's.

I pick up an unused notebook and a blue pen. *How to Survive a War*, I write. *One: Name the war. Two: Who is fighting? Three: What is lost? Four: Who wins? Five: Who survives?*

A war is not a thing that happens on its own, where the people are incidental. The reasons for war are the tinder; those who fight are the embers, the ash. If no one comes back, it's as if they walked into fire and were consumed—with no trace, no memory, no one to say what happened in the blaze. And surviving is not just coming out alive but being able to *live* again. This is the whole point.

I don't have to wait for Ambuya to talk; these things they saved will tell me. The box at my feet holds not only memories, but lives—Ambuya's, the gogos', maybe even Mama's. Perhaps understanding where their wars began will help me survive mine.

SEVEN

This time when Taren calls, I answer. I've been at Ambuya's almost a week now and Taren hasn't let up. It's precisely why I'm avoiding her; she's exhausting and I'm already beyond.

"Yeah!" I snap.

"Why have you been ignoring me?"

"What do you want, Taren?"

"I want to talk to you. You're my sister and you've been ignoring me."

"Maybe I'm not your sister, have you thought about that?"

"Of course you're my sister! You're being selfish. How do you think *we* feel?'"

"At least you have two parents. I have one and a bio donor."

"Stop being sorry for yourself and be Chianti. All that other crap doesn't change who you are. And it doesn't change anything for *us*. Mama and Baba aren't part of our sisterhood, they're just in charge and they're doing a poor job of it. It's not only you who's mad—everyone's upset."

"Kiki?" It's Tisha, in the background. "We miss you."

I don't say I miss them too. I don't have room for it. I stay quiet.

"It's okay," she says, "I know you miss us. You don't think so because you're upset. We don't like it here, we want to go home, will you come too? Or are you going to stay and go to school there? We've got another three weeks or so to go . . ."

Oh my gosh! Tisha is draining me rapidly. "This is why I didn't want to talk," I say. "I can't think about all that right now."

"Don't hang up!" Taren says frantically. "Wait!"

I wait. There's silence.

"Don't hang up," she says again, calm. I don't hang up. We don't speak.

Finally, I say, "Did you tell anyone? At school? Petra?" Petra is Taren's best friend. She's got her own issues. She has no business in ours.

"No!" Taren says. "Why would I tell anyone? And anyway, what if it's not true and Mama was just being mean?"

"It's true," I say. Even Mama is not that mean.

"They need to do a DNA test," Tisha calls out.

"Then they should do it on all of us," Taren declares.

I hear Tisha gasp at the idea that the situation might apply to them too. A small laugh starts inside me but doesn't come through.

"Realistically," Taren continues, "it's only the mother who knows the father of her children. And sometimes even she isn't sure."

I don't like what this might say about Mama, even though I'm mad at her. "Don't say things like that," I tell Taren.

"Where's the lie?"

"Well, see what the truth got us."

"Because first it was a lie, that's why," says Taren. "Did she tell you?"

"Tell me what?"

"Who."

"Who what?"

"You know," she says. "You know!"

"No, she didn't."

Taren lets out a loud breath on the other end of the phone. "Do you want to know?" she asks but doesn't wait for me to answer. "I don't want you to know, I don't want you to have another family. Baba is your dad and we're your sisters."

Tisha does backup.

"He hasn't even called me," I point out. "I don't think he wants to be my dad anymore."

"We hardly see him so he might as well not be our dad either. He just dumped us here with old Cotton-Gusset Full-Broeks!"

I pack out laughing. "If Ambuya Minana hears you calling her that, you'll be washing dishes for a month."

"We already are!" Tisha calls.

"Lucky you, you got the fun granny," Taren grumbles.

"Yeah, but I don't feel very fun lately."

"You should call Baba and tell him," Tisha says.

"Tell him what?" I ask her.

"Tell him that it doesn't matter what Mama said. You've been his daughter all along—why should that change?"

"It's not just words," I say. "It's a matter of blood."

"What about kids who are adopted?" Taren asks.

"Well, they know they're adopted."

"Not always," she fires back. "What about when they haven't been told? What does blood matter then?"

"It matters."

"Bullcrap!" Taren says emphatically.

"Taren!"

"Bull. Crap!" she says again and starts to cry.

I don't want to talk anymore, but I stay on the line and listen to Taren until she stops. "Okay," I say, "I've got to go."

"Okay," she says, sniffing.

"Okay." I end the call.

Lying on my bed, staring at the ceiling, I think about blood. Bloodlines matter here. You belong to your father's family, so if Tinashe stays my father, it's a thing made of paper. Blood speaks, and that's what holds water.

Maybe I resemble my father. I always thought I looked like Tisha and Taren, but maybe I didn't have a reason to see otherwise. Taren and Tisha don't care now, but what if we have a disagreement and they form an alliance against me? I can't count on Mama; she's their mother too. What will I do?

I'm breathless, sick to my stomach. I want to cry but I can't. I roll over and put my head on my knees, and I heave and heave.

Ambuya is smart. I see now why she was made an ambassador. At dinner, when I ask her again about Sekuru, she says, "Oh, that's a story that needs me to be sitting down to tell you." She is sitting down, but I translate it to mean *when I'm not eating.*

After we finish supper she must sense that I'm about to ask again, because she says, "I don't want to have to retell it when Taren and Tisha ask, so I will tell you when you're together."

"Oh, but Ambuya, when will that be?"

"My dear, there's no rush. The story isn't going anywhere."

"Is it because you don't want to talk about the war?"

"It's because I don't want to have to tell the story twice." There's a warning in her voice. She may be fun and stylish, but she's no pushover.

"Gogo Ropa told me she went to war when she was seventeen."

Ambuya's cup of tea stops short of her mouth. "Gogo Ropa talked to you about the war?"

"Yes," I say, hoping the change of tactic might give me results.

"What did she say?"

"She showed me her scars from the crawling she had to do. Do you have them too?"

She takes a sip of her tea and watches me over the rim of her cup. "Not anymore," she murmurs.

"How did you get rid of them? Gogo Ropa said they were lifelong."

"Hmm!" she says. "For others. For me, sheer willpower did the trick."

"They weren't badges of honor for you?"

"In a way," she says, "but that was just the beginning of the scars. Better the ones you can ease away with oils and creams." She puts down her teacup and begins to round up the plates, pushing them to me. "Have you called your father?"

"No." It doesn't occur to me to protest that he isn't my father.

"Maybe you should. He probably believes you're upset with him."

"He's the grown-up, shouldn't he be checking in on me?"

"He's a man," Ambuya says.

"Umm, that's a bit sexist, Ambuya."

Ambuya laughs. "Please! Don't talk to me about sexism. Fight a war first, come out of it and see if *sexism*"—she leans toward me and raises her eyebrows for emphasis—"is a problem men want fixed. No, my dear, men are just boys grown taller, with increased muscle mass. How else would you explain sugar daddies?" She taps a finger to her head. "*If you can keep your head when all about you are losing theirs . . . you'll be a Man, my son!*"

"What?"

"Rudyard Kipling. Poetry. What do they teach at that school of yours?" Ambuya asks as she exits, her silk caftan trailing behind her.

"They should teach us about avoidance tactics," I mutter. I've been played.

It's after ten when I pick up my phone and tap on Baba's number. A photo pops up; I'm standing in front of him, my head almost level with his chest. Tisha is on his back, peering around his shoulder, and Taren is holding on to his arm. It was taken before he started going to the gym, so his body is a bit round and soft. He still has his mustache, which I thought made him handsome. Everyone is smiling.

I like this photo. This is the Baba I would paint on a box. I'd sit him at a table in a shadowy restaurant, a spotlight on the singer he's watching onstage. He has no idea that life is about to give him a lemon.

Turned away from me, that man could be my bio dad. I only think it's Baba because that's what I know.

I don't like this story. I'll stick to seeing him on my phone for now.

The house is quiet, like an empty church. Even the frequent scurrying in the ceiling is absent. The silence amplifies my loud breathing. It's weird—I'm having a fight-or-flight response at the thought of calling my dad.

I sit up against the headboard and switch on my bedside lamp. It's Baba. He's not a stranger. He's the same man in the photo, who on that day took us to a friend's eighth birthday party and was the only dad having tea with the moms. Around that time, Mama's band had become famous and she was touring a lot. But Baba never let us miss anything. He would take us to a movie or for ice cream or to the supermarket for treats. He wasn't the most fun parent. He's a serious type of person. But we didn't mind that. We had Mama for zaniness and entertainment—we needed him to be the stable one. We didn't expect much from Mama except for her to be herself.

During a wild week when life felt tossed up and shaken about in our house, Baba surprised us. I was late for an out-of-town hockey game—I was the Under Thirteens captain that year—and no prizes for guessing why I was late. I was arguing with Mama about it when Baba grabbed my stuff, picked up his car keys, and said, "Come on! Are you going to stand there crying or are we going to try and get there?"

"I wasn't crying," I said as I jumped in the passenger seat. Tisha and Taren came running as the gate was opening and jumped in too. They started making a lot of noise to the tune of one of the cartoons they liked.

"Come on, Dad!" they yelled whenever we made it through a green light. "Green for . . . gooooooo!" We were all laughing but stopped when we arrived at school and were told the bus had left ten minutes before. Baba did a screeching turn and we were on our way again. "Catch that bus! Catch that bus!" Tisha and Taren chanted. I was too nervous to join in, but I was saying it in my head.

We caught up with the bus and Baba made them pull over. Mrs. Hatidii, the coach, was not impressed, but she let me get on and stay captain for the match. As the bus pulled onto the road, I peered out of the window. Baba's, Taren's, and Tisha's smiling faces were beaming at me as they waved. Baba honked twice and pulled away. I was proud of him that day. I was so happy.

hi Baba

it's me, Kiki

Of course he knows it's me. But maybe he's already deleted my number. Don't be silly!

. . . typing

Pause.

. . . typing

I make myself breathe in and out.

. . . typing

What on earth could he be typing? I watch the screen, waiting. And then—offline. No message comes through.

I'm breathing like I've run a race. My eyes are hot, but no tears come. I kick off the duvet and turn onto my side, staring at my phone. The screen locks, goes off. I don't move. I hold my breath. I wait for the ping.

EIGHT

It's early. The sun isn't up yet. I don't feel as if I slept. I woke with my phone right next to me. My eyes are gritty—maybe they didn't even shut, just in case I missed the text. But there's nothing. When I hear Ambuya moving around I get up and have a quick shower.

I don't say anything as I walk into the kitchen. Ambuya assesses the situation and makes the correct guess.

"I don't want to hear any complaining," she says as she puts her empty teacup in the sink.

I grab a bottle of juice from the fridge and put on my sneakers. Gogo Tapera is waiting in her old Land Rover at the gate.

"We spoiled Tamara," Gogo Tapera says.

"The back seat is awfully uncomfortable, Tapera—why

don't you buy another car?" Next to me, Gogo Stella is fidgeting. I agree, but my mouth doesn't open unnecessarily this time of morning.

"It's a classic," Gogo Tapera replies. "They don't make them like this anymore."

"*You* spoiled Tamara," Ambuya says from the front passenger seat. "You and Stella."

"Oh, she was the sweetest little thing," Gogo Stella coos. "I looked forward to when you couldn't take her with you and left her with me. You were always too hard on the girl, Precious."

"I had to balance you two. You let her get away with murder."

"No, Precious, it was not easy. Tamara was . . . strong-willed. I didn't have the . . ." Gogo Stella fumbles for the right word. ". . . skill . . . to manage that."

Ambuya turns around. "You brought down an enemy plane with an anti-aircraft missile but couldn't manage a little girl?"

"What about you?" Gogo Stella says. "You didn't manage so well yourself."

Ambuya kisses her teeth loudly and turns to face forward.

"What I'm saying," Gogo Tapera says, "is maybe we need an intervention."

"Oh! Is *that* what you were saying?" Ambuya laughs sarcastically. "Anyway, an anti-aircraft missile comes with instructions and is a piece of cake compared to Tamara."

All three women cackle and peace is restored.

"Maybe you should have . . ." Gogo Stella starts.

But Ambuya catches her unfinished thought with an air of finality. "Maybe nothing, Stella. I did the best I could."

There's no chance for further conversation because we arrive at the market.

Oh, the market! I'm Alice down the rabbit hole. We enter a warren of wooden structures with black plastic sheeting that creates a roof over each stand and forms a doomsday sky. There are clothes in huge heaps, handbags laid out on tables, shoes, busy people unpacking even more merchandise from bags; clothes and more clothes. The gogos move through the maze as if following a beacon.

The prelude ends and we are in the deep of things. The sounds of the edges fade away and there's a muted hum. The gogos separate; each has their own suppliers they deal with. I follow Ambuya. She stops at a cluttered stall full of shoes tied together with plastic bands in pairs—the nicer ones with only a single shoe on display.

"Winston, how are you this morning?"

"Gogaz, I'm well if you are well."

"I'm well. What have you got for me?"

He's a fairly young man, skinny, long arms and brown eyes with long lashes. He brings out a black bag full of shoes.

After a cursory glance through, Ambuya's steady gaze seems to say, *Still nothing?*

"Eesh!" He scratches his head. "Things are not okay, Gogaz. These thieves are ruthless. I haven't been able to restock since the last robbery. Yah, this is a big problem."

She sighs. "Any idea where the stolen bales are ending up?"

"I think they're going straight to Harare. Otherwise we would've heard murmurs." Winston scratches his head again. "I've had the same stock for the past two months and it's not moving. I need to mix it up with new inventory. It's tight, Gogaz."

"Hmm," Ambuya says. "Thank you, Winston."

We move from supplier to supplier. Most are not Ambuya's usuals. "You might unexpectedly strike gold," she says. She's in no hurry as she examines shoe after shoe after shoe. "If you see something you like, negotiate. If the wear and tear is not that bad, we can fix it." She hands me twenty dollars. "Don't pay more than five dollars for any used pair."

Ambuya has a cobbler who is a wiz at repairing and refreshing shoes. When I asked why they don't use him to make new designs, she said, "Where's the fun in that?"

It's hard work, is what it is. Dusty and hot. It's not easy to breathe under the plastic sky. I'm scared a fire might start in one of the narrow alleys. A burning rain of plastic flames, sticking to our hair and clothes and skin. Absolute horror.

"Hey!" Ambuya says. "Focus."

I've been standing lost in my disaster creation and running out of breath with every deadly scene. The vendor is watching me with questions in his eyes.

"Do you want those or not?" Ambuya asks.

I'm holding a cute pair of Miu Miu mules.

"If you don't, I'll take them. I already have plans for what I'll do with them."

I hold the shoes against me. "No, I'm taking them." It's not much of a negotiation—I pay five dollars because the heel is worn and can be fixed. They're not even appropriate for my age, but Ambuya isn't saying anything about it so neither will I.

I lose my sense of time as we wander from stall to stall. I'm exhausted, and it's as if I'm trying to breathe with a plastic bag around my head. No wonder Gogo Ropa doesn't come here. You need a certain kind of energy that only the other three seem to have.

When we finally return to the car, the sun is high. It's like we've emerged from a wormhole. I blink against the bright light and clutch my wares to my side. Ambuya has given me a cloth shopping bag to hold my purchases—the mules, a pair of almost new Converse high tops, and an unworn pair of vintage brogues. I must've sifted through a thousand pairs of shoes. I won't be doing it again in a hurry. Ambuya and the gogos are definitely soldiers—none of them look worse for wear.

Gogo Stella has had better luck. "I got a few American labels, and I have exciting ideas for the pieces that will come out. But this issue of the robberies has been going on long enough. We need to act sooner rather than later."

"True," Ambuya says. "We should strike once and keep it under the radar. Can't have the police and border officials turning their gaze on us. The routes the smugglers use are our home ground—no one knows them better than we do. Let's plan with that in mind."

“Apparently the robbers are getting more and more daring.” This from Gogo Tapera.

“Hmph! Then we need a daring approach,” Ambuya replies. “Just as well we’ve got surplus stock. Let’s focus on the handbags while we brainstorm our mission.”

I’ve seen the closetful of handbags they’ve stockpiled. They’re super designer with serial numbers. Gogo Tapera’s daughter takes them to America, has them repaired, and sells them online. I’m not allowed to talk about them to anyone.

Gogo Tapera changes gear to chug up the hill to Gogo Stella’s house.

“We need a strategy session,” Gogo Stella says.

“We need a drink,” says Gogo Tapera.

“It’s not even eleven o’clock,” says Ambuya.

“And you are saying . . . ?”

“I’m saying . . .” Ambuya smiles. “Blue, black, or Jack?”

All three burst out laughing. I’m not sure what’s funny, but I know they’re talking about whisky.

In her chaotic lounge, Ambuya Stella reveals the most massive bottle of whisky I’ve ever seen. Ambuya lets out a loud whistle and Gogo Tapera starts up with a high yipping sound. Then they’re singing and dancing. It’s a war song about the coming of the Chimurenga—the uprising. They’re wearing tracksuits and jogging up and down in formation, *toyi-toy*ing and chanting.

We’ve seen old footage in school of the guerrilla soldiers doing this during training. But it’s bizarre to see Ambuya like this now, when she’s usually measured and controlled. No wonder Mama is also unpredictable.

They seem like they're having a lot of fun, though. I almost want to join in.

They come to the end of their song, gasping and laughing, slap high-fives and fight to catch their breath. In the lull, I hear the noisy birds in the garden. A tiny yellow-breasted bird flies in, straight out of a tree, as the door opens.

Gogo Ropa walks in, wearing fatigues and an olive-green tee. She closes the door behind her, assesses the situation, and issues a shrill, definitive whistle. The gogos come to attention and salute her. She barks an order and they begin another song in a circle, leaning in and clapping as they go.

I have no clue about the spark to this new flame, but they're in another time and place altogether. They've created a whole world for themselves.

I realize I have no idea who I am. I seem to have forgotten everything that came before. Maybe Mama's words did kill me.

NINE

"Hey, young lady, your attention, please." Mr. Kingsley Pfupajena is snapping his fingers in my face. I blink him into focus. We're on the bright patio outside his house. When I finally left the gogos, I told Ambuya I was going home for a nap, and she lifted her whisky at me and said, "Goodnight." It wasn't even one o'clock yet.

Outside, I stood looking up at Gogo Ropa's, wondering why she'd locked her gate when she was just next door. Now I'm here.

"I'm sorry. I didn't sleep well last night and was up early to go to the market. I'm a bit out of it."

"Oh, a day at market with those gogos will do it to you. I couldn't tell you where they find the patience and the energy."

"Maybe it's the whisky?"

He roars with laughter. "Did they tell you, 'Too much of anything is bad but too much whisky is barely enough?'"

"No, but they were *toyi-toy*ing around a giant bottle. Just seeing it gave them enormous joy."

"Aha!" Mr. Kingsley Pfupajena says. "I knew Stella took it, that sly creature. She swore up and down she never saw where it went." Seeing my expression, he waves his outrage away. "Never mind, never mind. But if you want me to keep it secret that you let that slip, we'd better get doing TikToks."

Inwardly I groan. I don't have the strength for this. Still, I know what damage misplaced words can do, so I agree. "But I'm hungry, Mr. Kingsley Pfupajena. Do you have anything to eat?"

"Yes, of course, my dear, come through."

His house is as much a treasure trove as Gogo Stella's. I'm guessing he gets more than just clothes when he goes to the market. There are books scattered about, old suitcases and trunks stashed in corners and used as end tables, vases and lamps of various makes and sizes, and framed sepia and monochrome photographs.

I notice a framed photo on the sideboard in the dining room. I see Ambuya straightaway. It's a wedding photo, but Ambuya is not the bride. The bride isn't wearing a white dress but a voluminous red creation under a short, embellished blue coat. She has a crown on her head and is holding long-stemmed orange and purple calla lilies. It's Gogo Stella, and Mr. Kingsley Pfupajena—fussy cravat and all—is the groom.

They're gazing at each other lovingly. I'm shook. "Mr. Kingsley Pfupajena!"

He pops his head around from the kitchen, where I heard him bumping pots and pans together. "Yes, dear?"

"You and Gogo Stella are married?"

"Not anymore," he says and pops back into the kitchen.

I follow him. This is unbelievable. "But that wedding picture—it doesn't look that old!"

"It's from when we renewed our vows. A year later we divorced."

The kitchen is like I've entered another house: clean and slick with gleaming granite counters and a huge gas range with lots of buttons and add-ons. There's a cozy booth in the corner with a vase of flowers and a picturesque window.

"Wow!" I take in the whole room. There are two shelves of cookbooks along one deep blue wall and gadgets everywhere.

"I like to cook," he says sheepishly.

"And Gogo Stella let go of a man who can cook?" I say, laughing. "Who would do that? What planet are you from?"

He winks at me and turns the pan in his hands with a flourish. "A fashionable one. I'm well ahead of my own existence. Come, sit down. I've poured you fruit juice."

He makes delicious eggs, bacon, toast, pancakes with ice cream and whipped cream, and fresh fruit salad. The ingredients come out of a big fridge and a pantry that looks like it's inspected by a drill sergeant each morning. I'm stuffed by the time we're ready to do the TikToks.

He drives me up the cul-de-sac to fetch a variety of "styles" from Gogo Stella and shoes from Ambuya. They join us for the video, which requires us to jump into shoes and change outfits. Gogo Tapera puts a little makeup on me and styles my braids. I feel like a zombie when we're finally done. I'm seeing everything as if from the next dimension.

But back at Ambuya's house, curiosity overpowers my fatigue.

In the storage room, I rummage through the photos again. I find some I've never seen before. These are shots of people posing in a photo studio in bell-bottoms and afros, in park-like gardens, in rural areas. I search for young Mr. Kingsley Pfupajena and Gogo Stella, more photos that could be part of their wedding. I'm also paying attention to any men who might be my grandfather. Surely in this box of memories, there would be a picture of Ambuya with a boyfriend or husband.

No matter how much I examine them, nothing signals—they mostly appear to be relatives or random strangers. All the same, I slip a couple of prospects into my notebook.

On a low shelf near where I'm sitting, I catch sight of an old box file with a rusted lock—the kind Taren would immediately try to open. I give it a halfhearted jiggle, but the small energy reserve that kicked in earlier decides not to hang around any longer. Sleep knocks on my eyes. I'll try again later.

As I crash onto my bed, it strikes me that Mr. Kingsley Pfupajena got away with telling me nothing about his marriage to Gogo Stella. *These old people are relentlessly cagey*, I think as darkness falls over me.

TEN

My phone shows it's nine o'clock. The birds outside my window are loud this morning. They must be Gogo Stella's, come to visit; ours are not this rowdy.

Tisha and Taren's shoebox is opposite my bed. I've stood it up longways like a phone. I glued their faces—cutouts that I drew in pencil—onto a colorful background full of emojis, with cellophane to mimic a screen, and made the bottom half look like a keypad. This is my favorite box. It's fun, and I feel close to them without having to actually talk to them.

On the dining room table Ambuya has left me a vetkoek, a glass of milk, a few slices of cheese, and an orange. The message comes through as I sit down: ***Come to Gogo Stella's when you're ready.***

Two other texts came in while I was showering. Nothing from Baba. Has he disconnected himself from me? Like, just accepted the words as they were said and allowed them to be his new reality: *not your child*?

I'm Texting!!!!!

Taren is being sarcastic.

?????

Hi Kiki it's Tisha

Flower emoji, sun emoji, heart emoji

There's an emoji chain from Mama—a plane, a taxi, a South African flag, a hotel, *Zzzzs*.

Another ping. A voice note from Taren. I type: ***Will listen just now.***

I won't. I'm only interested in hearing from one person. Without him we'll never be able to fix what's been broken.

As I sit down to eat, the birds outside make a sudden racket, as if they're at a soccer match and the star player has scored a goal. A bright-blue bird streaks across the window. What on earth is happening? I get up to see but once I step out of the house, I find myself making my way to Gogo Ropa's. I don't know why I sense she will be home, I just do.

Her gate isn't open like last time, but it's not locked either. I raise the latch and close it after me. It's quiet here and even though I like the birds, I also like the quiet.

Gogo Ropa is different, like me. I'm part of a whole but not made up of the same everything as everyone else. If they were colors, the other gogos would be red, yellow, and orange, and Gogo Ropa would be blue. Taren and Tisha are yellow and orange, and I'm a red that's a lot like blue. In the earliest photos I've seen of them, from when they were kids together before the war, Gogo Ropa's eyes always look like they're seeing their own thing, while Ambuya and Gogo Stella are undeniably part of the same vision. I wonder what it is, the invisible thing that keeps Gogo Ropa in her own space.

She's sitting in her car, which is parked by the side of the house. It's a Defender like Gogo Stella's, an old one, in olive green.

"What are you doing sitting here, Gogo?" I ask, leaning up against the window on the driver's side. "Did you guys get these like a package after the war or what?" I'm only half joking.

Gogo Ropa laughs, but with no joy. "That would've been marvelous, wouldn't it? Get in."

I go around to the passenger side and climb in. "Are we going somewhere?"

"Can you drive?" she asks, staring ahead of us into the backyard, which is as tidy and open as the front. There's a cottage with a washing line, but no clothes on it, no activity from the cottage. These gogos are strange in that they don't have anyone working for or living with them.

"You can't trust people," she says, as if reading my mind. "You have to watch what you say and do. Anyone can be secretly working against you."

In a moment of bitterness, I think, *Even your own mother!*

"People from our village blamed me for leading Precious and Stella into war. If only they knew how much I tried to convince them to return. They're such stubborn girls—younger by a year or two, but always trying to do what I did. At first I was angry with them for not listening to me, but eventually I understood."

She puts both hands at the top of the steering wheel and leans forward, staring into the yard. It's almost too quiet, like we've disappeared into the absence of sound and become just breath and heartbeat.

"What was it like?" My voice feels too loud, but Gogo Ropa hasn't heard me. I clear my throat and try again. "I mean, what kind of things did you have to do after the training? When you had to fight."

"Fighting . . ." She says nothing else for a long while. "No. Don't fight if you don't have to. Be the unseen. Appear when they least expect it." She turns to me. "You want to learn about war? Come and find me."

Gogo Ropa doesn't wait. She jumps out of the car, slams the door shut, and makes her way toward the cottage. I shake off my sluggishness and follow.

Behind the cottage I come to a stop. As far as my eyes can see there are trees leading to a grayish mountain in the distance, cloaked in mist. It's not a bright day, but heat is seeping through the haze. Gogo Ropa is nowhere to be seen. I notice where she's brushed aside a branch, and I know she did that on purpose so I can follow.

I don't stop to be afraid. I'm excited, imagining this is what it felt like in the war—but not as dangerous, of course. It's been a while since I felt it was okay to just do a thing and not have a hundred thoughts helter-skeltering through my mind. I plunge into the foliage with zeal.

Flying things, stinging things, roots and clumps clutter the path. I pass stones, boulders, rotting leaves, mud and singing things, birds that flit and call out, sunlight in and through branches, fallen logs, the sound of rushing water, and I stop.

I wasn't afraid before, I'm not afraid now. In a sense I've disappeared. The world doesn't have to exist outside of this. I'm uncomfortable, feeling untethered, but I remind myself I'm not alone. Where is Gogo Ropa? The ground has been gradually sloping down, and now I'm in a deep, leafy arbor. It smells damp and murky. I'm breathing fast and sweating.

Out of nowhere, Gogo Ropa grunts.

If a person could jump out of their skin, that's what I do. I scream as if I'm being murdered, holding on to a tree so hard I'm surprised I don't snap the trunk in two. All I can see at first are the whites of her eyes in a bushy creeper growing up the tree.

"Gogo Ropa!" I shout. "Why?"

She comes into focus, sitting on a fallen log in her full camouflage. "You would never survive a war," she says with a shake of her head. "Shame. It's just as well we did the fighting for you."

I can't speak because I might be sick. My vision is blurry and my breath is skipping.

"You sounded like a wounded rhinoceros crashing through the bush, not caring that you might be ambushed," she goes on. "I would've died if not for my stealth. I was famed for it. They called me Chipoko. That was my war name. Hokoyo Chipokouyo: Beware the Ghost. It had a nice rhyme to it. We even sang it as a song." Goga Ropa laughs. It's the first time I've heard her laugh, and she sounds rusty.

My legs have had enough. I take a seat next to her.

"I don't regret it," Gogo Ropa says. "I never would've gotten that chance to be my true self if I'd stayed and done my duty for the family. It would've been death by degrees, gradual but sure."

As she speaks, she has the same sitting-in-a-chair-in-a-semidark-room-sipping-whisky energy as the last time I saw her.

"The man I was supposed to marry, he was much older, stern. He scared me. Imagine being more scared of a man than of war. I realized then that I wasn't scared of a man—I was scared of never being free. I survived hunger, I survived grueling physical demands on my body, I survived bombs and armed combat, because I chose freedom. I knew I had everything to live for, so I fought as if all my tomorrows had been promised. Can you imagine what it's like to know that with every single fight, you're fighting for everything? No runners-up, no consolation prizes."

"Do you feel free?" I ask her.

"I am free," she says simply. "Feelings and thoughts are another matter."

"What does it mean to you, to be free?" I ask. The sound of water nearby makes me thirsty.

"If you have to ask me that," she says, "you don't yet understand freedom."

"I get that I'm not free," I say glumly. "I'm bound by the words and actions of my parents. I'm bound by the rules of my school. I'm bound by my responsibilities and obligations to my younger sisters. I'm bound by everything."

"We are all bound. If one of us is not all right, none of

us are all right. People have lost sight of this." She taps her chest. "In here, free." Taps her head. "Not free. Freedom is not a thing outside of self, but the world will never allow you to remember that."

Gogo Ropa's voice increases in intensity as she speaks, as if she wants to imprint the words on my mind, like she might grab me by the shirt-front and shake them into me. Her eyes, behind the smudges, are fierce and bright as she looks into that place only she can see.

"Do you know what your gogos were famous for during the war?" Gogo Ropa asks in an abrupt turn of conversation. She leans away to give me back my space.

"No," I say. "Ambuya hardly ever talks about the war."

"You should ask them," she says with a hint of a smile. "But if you think about it, you'll guess, and it wasn't for their fashion sense."

This makes me laugh as scenarios flash before my eyes. I can only imagine they must've been totally outrageous, given that so much was unheard of for young women in those days. I ran away to the safety of my grandmother's house; they ran away to a whole war.

"Was he a bad man? Your father?" I ask Gogo Ropa.

"No, he was just a man who believed what he knew. It was his duty to do what had to be done."

"Did he love you?"

Her eyes, through the camouflage, lock on to me and for a moment it's spooky, like a bush has come to life and is beaming into my soul. I feel winded and a little trapped. I think of the rocket launcher.

“Love,” she says, as she stands up, barely shaking the leaves around her. She turns away.

I make the mistake of blinking and find myself alone. Only the sounds around me continue: cicadas, gurgling water, birds, buzzing insects.

A bush several feet away moves and says, “Love is just a word, until it’s put into action.”

ELEVEN

I haven't thought much about who my real father could be. I've been obsessed with getting the one I had back.

My real father could be anyone. Am I ready for that? It's a no for me, as Tisha would say. There are too many possibilities. Maybe he's a famous musician, or the president of a small country. Maybe he's a fake pastor in one of those churches in a suburb. Maybe he's alive or maybe he's dead. Maybe he's rich or poor, maybe he's someone else's father and has no clue I exist. Maybe he's aware of me and doesn't care. Maybe he's searching for me . . .

But I don't love him. He's never done anything for me.

At school, we once had to write an essay on what home meant to us. I spent three days writing how home is where your family lives, where you are safe, a place you know more than any other. After I got a B minus, I realized that home is a feeling. Tinashe is not the most exciting dad, he's not even the best dad, but I'm always happy to go home to him. Even when there's fighting, I know where to take cover, and even though we hate it when it happens, it's a feeling we're used to.

My heart is beating in my tongue. One of us needs to be brave and press the button. I'm holding my phone, ready to call. But if Baba doesn't answer I will be so upset and if he does answer and he's not nice, I'll be even more upset. The level of upset I am right now is more than enough.

The clock changes to 00:00 as I'm holding my phone, staring at my lock screen. It has a photo of me, Taren, Tisha, Mama, and Baba standing at the top of Domboshava Rock, high above Harare, a blue sky with fluffy clouds behind us. We're smiling and holding up our arms to show off our muscles. This was one of the last days before the war in our house began.

I saw then that Baba enjoys hiking and outdoor things, and this is when I've seen him with real pep. Putting on suits and ties must take that away, and that's why he hasn't always seemed like much fun. His suits and ties are a parasite. Shame—the gogos fought a war against colonial oppression only for their children to be oppressed by a way of life. When they were fighting, maybe they knew what they would do with that freedom, but when they got it, they started to waffle.

It seems I've been thinking for forever, but the clock only changes now. 00:01. One minute has passed. We used to call it a kind of magic to see the clock change, especially at midnight. We competed to see who could stay up longest to catch that crucial lapse when time becomes no time, when the whole world is holding its breath until it becomes the next day. Of course it's not the same everywhere at once, but it feels that way when it's your turn for midnight.

My stomach rumbles. I can't remember if I ate supper; the day's been such a jumble. I go to the kitchen. It's like I have a rowdy kid tumbling around, banging the skin of my stomach, playing a drum. Ambuya never wakes me to eat or do stuff. It was nice at first to be left alone, but I'm worried I'll lose all sense of real life. Mama doesn't operate like that in our house, where there's a strict order. It's strange, but I'm beginning to miss it. I'm freefalling here.

I don't see Ambuya sitting in the armchair until I walk by with my plate. It should startle me to death, but it doesn't. She's not asleep; she's staring into the empty fireplace.

"Go on to bed," she says.

"I'm not sleepy." I walk to the other armchair and sit facing the same way. It's cool at night here but not so much that a fire is needed. I bite into my cheese and ham sandwich. Ambuya breaks off a piece of chocolate and puts it on my plate.

"I'm surprised you're still up. It was busy today at Gogo Stella's," I say.

"Hmm, it's always busy. I don't sleep much."

"How come?" I ask.

She shrugs. "Have you heard from your mother?"

"Yes, she's in Jo'burg." I don't explain that it's not hearing from her exactly, but receiving emoji chains by text.

"Tisha and Taren miss you," Ambuya says.

"I know."

"This whole thing has affected them too. It doesn't change the fact you're still their sister and they love you."

"I'm not the one who took them away," I say.

"It's not their fault."

"Whose fault is it, Ambuya?" I've been trying not to think about it, much less talk endlessly. "How come you won't answer my questions about Mama's dad?"

"He died before the war ended," Ambuya says.

It sounds convenient. She could've told me when I first asked. I get the impression Ambuya is not being completely honest, but I still have fully functioning brain cells so I keep my opinion to myself.

"I'm technically an orphan," Ambuya announces. "I never felt like one growing up, though. I had a family. Most were great, a few not so much, and that was life. It was the same throughout. No one had a perfect life of their own—a mother, a father, a house. My parents, the ones who made me, drowned while crossing a flooded river. I missed them, but things continued on the homestead. We were all children together and the adults were a conglomeration of mothers, fathers—junior and senior and elders. It didn't matter whose house you ate at, which house you slept at. There was no 'your house, your mom, your dad,' there was just home. Everyone had their part to play and that's how it worked. Decisions about the children were made by the family. It wasn't always fair or desirable, especially if the father in charge was a hard man . . ."

"And that's why you ran away to fight," I say, biting

into the square of chocolate. "What were you and Gogo Stella known for?" I ask, remembering my conversation with Gogo Ropa.

At this, Ambuya smiles and gets a distant look in her eyes. "We sang."

At first, I think she's being funny and doing her avoidance tricks.

But she leans forward and says, "It's true. Song and dance were used to raise the morale of the troops at political activation meetings. Myself and Stella, we could sing and dance through the night, and we were electric with it. At the parade grounds during drills, we reminded the recruits why they were there."

I'm not surprised; they've still got that charge. "But you didn't just sing and dance the whole time," I say. "I mean, when you left home, was that what you thought you were going to do?"

Ambuya doesn't answer immediately. "We left home to fight for freedom for our country, for ourselves. We were young. We had no idea what that would entail. We only knew it had to be done."

Wanting to sound clever, I say, "It's ironic, isn't it, Ambuya, that freedom isn't free?"

"My dear, freedom of any kind comes with a price, often a steep one."

"Gogo Ropa . . ." I say. "Did something bad happen to her?"

Ambuya turns to study me briefly before responding. I hold my breath.

"You leave her be," she says. "She treasures her peace and quiet. She's earned it."

I want to say, *So peace and quiet can be earned, but freedom isn't real,* but there's a limit to the amount of clever comebacks I can get away with.

I've been finding the unlimited freedom I've been given a bit unbalancing. Now, when I think of the gogos running away from unwanted marriages, I think of myself running away from the consequences of my mother's marriage—and I find it funny we all left home. Or "changed location," as Gogo Ropa would say. I guess sometimes home is a feeling you choose to leave behind.

What I'm beginning to understand is there are levels to the illusion of freedom, and once you are afraid—of anything—you have no hope of being free. When this is over, I worry the fracture we've suffered in our family will remain unhealed.

And Mama? Was her desire to be free from the lie greater than her fear of the consequences? A balancing act for which she didn't bother with scales? Maybe for her it was worth it, a sigh of relief, a subjective freedom.

TWELVE

I must've fallen asleep on the sofa. I have a crick in my neck. I hear Ambuya moving around in the kitchen and I make my way to her. We say our good mornings.

"Don't think I didn't try and get you to move from that sofa, because I did," she says, wiping down the sink. The kitchen is flooded with light and it's almost too bright. "I can sense the accusation from the way you're rubbing your neck. I told you to go to bed and you refused."

So much for wanting structure. "Sorry, Ambuya," I say.

She shrugs. "I'm not the one who's suffering. Here." She hands me a cup of milky tea.

I take a seat at the kitchen table. There's a plate with a peanut butter sandwich on white bread and a banana.

"Eat," she says as she sits down with her own cup.

"You're not going to the market today?"

"There's no point. Nothing's come through. We're working on a plan for what to do. We can't very well go to the police about these bales being stolen when they've technically been banned."

"If it's illegal, why are you doing it?"

"Often these decisions are not well thought out. They're more to do with politics, and the people are forgotten."

"But the law is the law," I say.

"Until it's in someone's interest to change it. Meanwhile people have to eat."

"You gogos don't seem to be suffering from impoverishment," I say. "Why do you do it? You've been an ambassador out of the country."

At this Ambuya scoffs. "My dear, the same meat that made you fat last year will make you sick today. Things change. Not to say we earned much as diplomats or ever got meaningful war compensation, but if you're not at work producing goods you can sell, you will starve. We were fortunate that we stayed in this part of the country. Had we tried to live in the capital, things would be worse for us. But we stumbled on the opportunity to buy this land in the late eighties. We put our money together and built our houses. In those days there was still sanity to the economy—you could do things with what you had. Now!" She shakes her head and sips her tea. "You're not old enough to fully understand life outside of a walled garden, but you have eyes and ears."

I know, and I feel bad that I don't really care. My world is topsy-turvy, but there's a nagging fear of finding myself outside the walled garden and fending for myself. Would I care about laws then, if I had to make money for rent and food? If Mama doesn't get her act together and Baba abandons me and Ambuya is not there, what would I do?

My feelings must be written on my face because Ambuya changes the subject.

"I spoke to your mother this morning. She returns from South Africa in a few days. I doubt she'll be in a rush to see me, so I'm sure you're here for the duration."

My heart does a twisty dance in my chest. I hum an answer into my cup and taste nothing. There's a bit more than a couple of weeks of summer break left, and I'm in no hurry to spend that time at home.

"How come she doesn't stay here when we visit?" I ask.

Ambuya sighs. Her copper bracelets jangle as she lays her arm across the table and picks at the edge of a mat. "Your mother, she's complicated. I guess she needed a more stable environment to grow up in. What did we know about raising a child, other than our own childhood? Stella was the most stable of us, with Mr. Kingsley Pfupajena for a while, but I suspect we only confused her—unconventional people trying to give a child a conventional life. She's angry about a lot of things. I acknowledge where I made mistakes, but I don't think I was a bad mother. I loved her, we all did, we all do. It doesn't appear to be enough for her presently and that's okay."

I'm surprised she's said this much. She must be tired from the late night and not on her A game in diplomatic vagueness. I reach out and take her hand. I put it against my face.

"I love you, Ambuya," I say. "You confuse me too

sometimes, but it's fun here and I'm glad I came." I must be a bit punch-drunk myself. A flash flood of love for my grandmother takes me under.

She takes my face in both her hands and leans over to plant a smacking kiss on my nose. "Muzukuru wangu," she says. *My grandchild.* A statement and an endearment.

It's only at Gogo Stella's while I'm pulling shirts apart at the seams that I realize Ambuya outmaneuvered me. She knew I was heading for more questions and neatly summarized what she was prepared to give, issuing a press statement that changed my focus. I see why Mama might be permanently mad at her. But she's my gran and that means I can give her latitude. Plus, she's my sanctuary. I don't have room to be angry at any more people.

After Mr. Kingsley Pfupajena has made me do the one hundred and sixtieth take of a fast-change dance TikTok, I need to escape outside for a breather. They all have much more energy than I do. Strangely, they don't seem old. They don't worry much either; even the problem with their suppliers has given them an exciting new project to work on.

They've agreed to plan a stealth mission against the robbers that would leave no trace of their involvement. Gogo Tapera is reactivating her knowledge of the unofficial routes through the bush from her secret agent days. Back then, she was crossing borders undetected, so this, by comparison, should be a simple feat.

I want to hear more about the war, but will Mr. Kingsley Pfupajena give me a minute to myself? I start edging away as they discuss taking over the town and running it themselves, but decide it would be too hectic and that there's not enough whisky in the world to help them deal with that kind of stress.

By the time I finally slip out, they're having a memory-lane session about "Jacket," a freedom fighter whose life was saved by the very jacket he'd been told to discard because it smelled so bad, which was what ultimately deterred the enemy.

They're laughing uproariously, surrounded by the remains of the lunch Gogo Stella served—sadza, knucklebone, and fried greens with a spicy relish on the side. Gogo Stella gave me Cherry Plum soda in a can and then they all requested one and drank like they'd never tasted it before.

The storage room has become a kind of refuge for me. I've laid out the photos in order of dates, putting those with family I recognize in one section, those from the war in another, and those from the same period in another. The floor is a mosaic of pictures, framed by letters, newspaper clippings, and other assorted papers—notes and official typewritten reports from army bases, records of people, food stores, munitions.

The work I've done feels purposeful. I haven't read through every document—there are too many and a lot of them are boring—but I remember the box file. For once I'm grateful for Taren's misdemeanors. I learned how to get behind locks from watching her: sheer determination and a sharp tool.

Impatience wins the day, and the lock comes apart after vigorous prying with a metal spoke. Not worth the bother, or the trouble I might get for breaking into it, when all I find is a leatherbound notebook with missing pages. I don't want to risk Ambuya catching me, so I tuck it into the waistband of my jeans. I'll read it in my room later. I return the file to the shelf, with the busted lock facing the wall.

Outside, the birds are flitting from bush to lawn to flowerbed to branch. They're ridiculously colorful—greenish blue, aquamarine, yellow, orange—flit, flit, fly, flit, flit, fly. Every time I see the birds, Gogo Ropa and her bright eye shadows come to mind.

When I walked past her gate earlier it didn't appear locked. Ambuya said to leave her be, but talking to her might give me answers. I've learned more about Ambuya's family from Gogo Ropa and the photographs in the spare room than I ever have from Ambuya herself.

Even though they're close and have been through the most together, Gogo Ropa is different. Ambuya and Gogo Stella are her blood family, like Taren and Tisha are mine. They shared a life before the war, but something separates them still. Maybe if I find out more about it, I'll figure out what made Mama the way she is, and it might help me be okay with my situation.

THIRTEEN

The gate isn't locked, so I go in. There's an eerie stillness. Last time I came, a tiny orange bird greeted me, and I almost expected it to be there again today, but it's not. I should be able to hear the birds from Gogo Stella's, but when I stop to listen, there's nothing.

I'm uneasy, which surprises me, as I didn't feel that way before. There was an instruction in Ambuya's words from last night that translated to *Don't go bothering Gogo Ropa at her house*. I brush it aside as I approach the door. It's slightly open, and I call out my knock.

There's no reply. Maybe she's busy inside and doesn't hear me. I take it that since the door is open, I can enter.

The curtains are half-drawn, creating an atmosphere of gloom in the living room. Papers and books are strewn over the table where the computer sits, monitor off. I wander through to the kitchen, calling out, but silence meets me. I head down the hallway to the bedrooms. All the doors are closed except the one at the end—I guess that's the master bedroom.

"Gogo Ropa, it's me, Chianti." I should probably leave, but now I worry something is wrong. What if Gogo Ropa has had an accident in the bathroom and is unconscious? What if she fell off her bed and broke a bone and can't cry for help? What if a thief surprised her from the garden where it's wild with trees? I approach quietly and slip inside.

The curtains are closed, but through the light from the ensuite bathroom I see the room clearly. A single mattress is pushed into the far corner, and the only things on it are a sheet and a thin blanket. The air is stuffy, and in a corner there is a stockpile of tinned goods and bottles of water. Flashlights of different sizes and packages of batteries are piled neatly beside them. The parquet flooring is polished to shine like a mirror under my feet. All this is not what I'd expected, but what catches and holds my attention is the back wall of the room.

The small windows at the top are taped down with the type of brown paper we covered our notebooks with in middle school. The breeze-block holes are stuffed, shutting out light and air, and the entire wall is plastered with scribbled writing, photos, drawings and clippings from magazines and newspapers.

A sensation of cold water running through my body makes me shiver. My breath hitches. At first it's difficult to decipher the writing; there are names, many I haven't come across before, but I pick out Precious and Stella Mapfumo—Ambuya and Gogo. Their names come under the word *Batmen*, underlined. From papers at Ambuya's I've read about them being batmen at the women's training camp in Chimoio. They were young when they joined, so they were assigned to do chores for senior officers. I've seen a photo of them smiling in fatigues, standing with buckets by an outdoor tap.

Gogo Ropa's wall is an advanced and palpable version of my floor mosaic.

Columns of names surround a field of crosses with *758+ DEAD* in a circle. There's a site map—squares clustered together, trees, open areas where stick figures stand in rows and armored trucks run over other figures with their hands up—next to a picture torn from a magazine, of bodies piled into a gaping hole in the ground. There are names scribbled above the drawings: *Chimoio 77, Nyadzonya 76.*

The reports and records in Ambuya's box of memories are coming to life in my head. I remember reading how a rogue fighter led the enemy into a refugee camp at Nyadzonya and there was a massacre. How bases in Chimoio were bombed in an unexpected air raid when paratroopers chuted in and it was a disaster.

All along, the notes, documents, and photos I came across in that box have felt like bits of stories I'd learned from history books. But now, it's as if I've passed through and into Gogo Ropa's mind. The pieces are a jigsaw puzzle showing that war is not just a word for a space in time. War is lists of names and numbers of the dead, it's blurry spots in your head and memories that won't stay in order.

Everything is in black and white, even the photos, and I wonder if Gogo Ropa decided this consciously, as if putting together an art installation. There are scribbles of calculus and quotes about the Boston Tea Party and Winston Churchill. Long wavy lines form a river in which stick figures drown, while on the bank, other figures hold stick guns. I don't recognize anyone in the photos—most are too grainy to pick out faces—but the AK-47 rifles and the belts carrying bullets are easy to spot. I'm filled with a deep sadness, as if I'm there with them.

I spot the scribbled chorus from a song I've heard the gogos singing, and I see them now, laughing, without a care in the world. But standing before Gogo Ropa's wall, I've stumbled into her silences and the reason Ambuya doesn't answer questions. No wonder they don't talk about things. It seeps sorrow into your bones and pulls you into the gloom.

The black scribbles mesmerize me, like the wall wants to whisper the things it knows and make me a part of it. I imagine the writing peeling off, swirling around me, the drawings and photos wrapping themselves tight and holding me hostage. In the corners of my vision, the room grows dim and the wall begins to grow . . .

I come to with a jolt, as if emerging from a tangle of smothering blankets. In a panic I turn and run, down the hallway and out into light so bright that it blinds me.

I stop to catch my breath and get my bearings, and a stone falls to the ground at my feet. Then another one. And another, flying from the trees at the edge of the yard. It should spook me, but I'm still reeling from the revelation of being inside Gogo Ropa's head. I know it's her throwing the stones.

The minute I walk into the wild part of the garden, a thick bush at the base of a large msasa tree grabs me, and I find myself staring into her eyes.

"Precious!" She grips me by the shoulders and shakes me. "What are you doing here, Precious? Where is Stella? You must go home! Now! It's not safe."

"It's me, Gogo—Chianti," I manage, but I'm talking to myself. Her eyes never waver. They're looking but she doesn't see.

"Come, I'll show you the way. It's not safe, we're surrounded. Rhodesian paratroopers landed not far from here."

My heart is beating wildly. Her grasp is powerful and I know I've once again found myself in a situation I cannot control.

Gogo Ropa is a fever of action, and I don't understand how she's this strong. As she drags me deeper into the trees I wonder if I should resist or just hope she snaps out of it. In my head I'm telling myself, *It's okay, it's just Gogo Ropa's yard, I'll find the house.*

But I'm not alone in my head. My heart is in there too, and it's saying, *Chianti, this is bad, what if she doesn't snap out of it? What if she disappears and leaves you where there are wild animals? The Gabon viper is found in these parts—that's certain death.* And this is what gives me strength to pull free and run.

Tears prick my eyes and things fly into my mouth until I break out coughing and run headfirst into something hard and unyielding. I can't hold a single thought as everything becomes loose inside. I'm trying to figure out if I'm standing or swinging upside down like a pendulum when I feel dry grass stabbing me. I'm on the ground. Darkness falls.

FOURTEEN

I wake up in a strange bed with four solemn faces watching me. The sun through the window is torture. Mr. Kingsley Pfupajena, by my bedside, is in a tracksuit with a doctor's coat over it, a stethoscope around his neck.

I'm floating. My throat is sore, my stomach is hollow, and my head hurts. There's a drip attached to my arm. Mr. Kingsley Pfupajena shines a light into my eyes and does doctorly things before moving aside to write on a clipboard. The gogos are silent.

Ambuya reaches over to stroke my face. "Chianti, we're sorry. No one paid attention when you left. We should've been watching you."

I want to ask her what happened, but my voice is lazy and my eyes don't care about seeing, so they close.

I'm plowing through brush and branch like an elephant on a drunken marula spree. I don't hear Gogo Ropa behind me. I have to get help. No, I'm not Precious, I'm Chianti, and today has gone terribly wrong. There are Rhodesian paratroopers in the area. I have to find safety. No, it's a Gabon viper, but we're not in Gabon. This is bad, Chianti, don't run to Mozambique by mistake! Stop running, no, get help, something's in my mouth—*Bam!*

My eyes flash open, my body jerks all the way up, my hand flies to protect my head even though it's too late—I've already hit it into blackness.

The room is in shadows now. Four solemn faces are still watching me. I'm breathing heavily and coughing, choking on whatever I imagined was in my mouth. Mr. Kingsley Pfupajena and Ambuya lay me back on the bed and doctorly things happen again. Every time I open my eyes, Ambuya and the gogos are there. Mr. Kingsley Pfupajena too. It's the quietest they've been and I don't like it. It makes me want to cry. *You don't cry,* I tell myself.

It's the hushed part of the night when my voice finally finds me. Only Ambuya is here now. She's wide awake, staring into the dim light. I clear my throat, and she sits up to give me a sip of water. It's cool but makes me nauseous when it hits my stomach. I don't drink any more.

"What happened, Ambuya?" My voice is a whisper.

"Why am I here?" I've used up every ounce of energy just saying those words.

Ambuya sighs. "Rest now. We'll talk about it tomorrow when you're fully awake."

"I'm awake now," I say, though it's as if my body is being pulled by a huge magnet inside the earth. My eyes are wide open and I don't want to sleep. "Did I bang my head against a tree? Was it a dream?"

Ambuya reaches out and takes my hand. "We didn't think it would come to this," she says. "Maybe we should've told you, but it's never been a problem before and we put measures in place. Mr. Kingsley Pfupajena . . ."

"A doctor?" I ask. "Did I dream him as a doctor?"

"No, you didn't dream it. He's a specialist physician but he doesn't practice much anymore."

This is far away from what I would've imagined him to be. I start to sit up. Ambuya props pillows behind me.

"Did I go on a wild run with Gogo Ropa and get knocked out?" In a brief snap of confusion, I imagine that a Rhodesian paratrooper was there and that he hit me with the butt of his gun. It's hard to get a handle on what's real.

The door creaks open and Gogo Tapera peeps in. Don't these old ladies ever sleep?

"She's awake?" she whispers. Gogo Tapera runs a smooth hand down my cheek before pulling me into a strong hug. I let my body fall into it until she leans me onto the pillows.

"She's asking about Ropa," Ambuya says to Gogo Tapera. They hold each other's gaze in silence.

"Yes," I say. "I went to see her, but there was this wall in her house and the stuff on it made my heart hurt. It was trying to be a part of me, so I ran outside." I give my head a little shake to clear the fuzz. "She made me run through the bush," I whisper. "Did she knock me out?"

"No, you ran into a tree and knocked yourself out," Ambuya says. "You scared us like nothing before has ever scared us."

"And Gogo Ropa? Did she carry me to the house?" My heart hammers painfully in my chest.

"When we found you, she'd managed to sling you over her shoulder. We choose to believe she was preparing to come to the house—otherwise we might've been searching for you forever. You can't find Ropa if she doesn't want to be found."

"She thought I was you," I say to Ambuya.

Ambuya and Gogo Tapera look at each other again, and annoyance flares up in my chest.

"What? For once, just tell me what I want to hear!"

Ambuya's eyebrow rises at this level of sass, but being in the hospital saves me. She takes a deep breath and squeezes both my hands. "Around this time of year, Gogo Ropa goes through . . . issues. We keep an eye on her but also try to give her space."

"She's back in the war, isn't she? In her head." I can't help it—I laugh, really loudly. I know it's hysteria because I can't stop. I let the laughter bubble and grow, until I groan with pain and I'm keening as if I'm at a funeral. There are no tears, only an ache that's too much to keep inside.

A nurse comes through the door and everyone is trying to calm me. The tears won't come to make it better, just the sounds I can't stop making. I feel a sharp prick, and hands lay me back. A warm current runs through me and I fall into a quiet place. I breathe a sigh of relief, and oblivion answers.

When I wake up to a bright morning, I've forgotten the midnight incident. Around lunchtime, I remember.

Ambuya is in the small bathroom, and Gogos Stella and Tapera are having a whispered conference by the door. What happened to Gogo Ropa? Is she still running and hiding in the bush?

On her wall of sorrows, there was a cross-section diagram similar to the ones we do in Geography. It showed trees and a tunnel that went straight into the earth and across, parallel to the ground above, then up again, a ways distant from the first tree. I see Gogo Ropa sitting there, hiding from paratroopers, waiting for the war in her head to end. I'm convinced that's where she is and it was a clever trick that let her disappear and move so fast.

But this isn't a magic show, or a long-ago history with monuments to tell us it happened. It's living, breathing, broken people who want to forget but who need to remember the people they can never get back to. It's not that my problems aren't problems and don't compare. It's not that they can't scar me; they have. But I'm only a bit broken.

The warmth trickling down my face comes before it registers that I'm crying. Twin tracks streaming into the pillow. *Two minutes*, my mind tells me. *Two minutes and be done with it.*

But soon I'm shaking and sobbing, and I can't stop. I can't make it quiet. I want to wash over everything with the tears until all that's left is bones and we can start again, getting the layers right.

FIFTEEN

It takes me a long while to calm down. In the end I force myself to stop because Ambuya and the gogos are aging in front of my eyes. They've come this far with the battles they've been through; I can't be the one to finish them off.

I eat the meal they've brought for me and smile through the puffiness of my face. Ambuya tells me they haven't yet called Mama and Baba. "Really, we should have," Gogo Stella says, but nobody wanted to.

"Tamara has such a temper," Gogo Tapera whispers, "and anyway, there's four of us and we can handle it. Mr. Kingsley Pfupajena is your dedicated doctor and you could ask for no better."

A part of me is laughing. Scared of Mama! But I understand; they're dealing with what they have on their plate instead of asking for an extra dollop of hot sauce.

And I'm relieved. I can't have Mama and Baba here

now. I don't know what more they'll bring with them, and I'm not ready for that. I can't say when I'll ever be ready.

Now that I'm on a break from crying, they tell me it was Ambuya's "famous sixth sense" that alerted them that something was wrong.

"It's true," Gogo Stella says, "Precious saved us many times during the war. We were about to wind up for the day when she stopped and got that faraway glint in her eyes. I knew immediately."

"Yes," adds Mr. Kinsgley Pfupajena, "and I was about to show you the latest reel I'd made, when we discovered you were nowhere to be found. We checked the perimeter cameras and saw you going into Ropa's."

"We'd seen the signs that Ropa was not herself," says Gogo Stella, "but we've been preoccupied with these damn robberies and didn't take our usual precautions. We forgot to factor you into the equation."

"True," Ambuya says. "I should've explained properly."

"You don't ever tell me anything!" I burst out, taking the opportunity to air my most pressing grievance.

Ambuya sighs and drops her head into her hand. "What could we possibly tell you that you would understand?" She rubs her forehead. "We knew nothing ourselves, going into war—we sang, we danced, we thought we were so brave. The training, grueling as it was, the hunger, the discomfort, even that was a far cry from what happened once bombs began falling and bullets took lives. War is hell. Death is not the end of breath or a final heartbeat. Death is . . . a ghost that haunts the living. Those it claimed are resting."

Silence follows Ambuya's words.

My complaint isn't wanting to know more about the war, just getting answers to my questions. But with Ambuya, you get what you get.

"It's not that we don't want to explain things. Every single day since meeting death, we're trying to forget it was there. If we pick things out for show and tell, there's a danger that much more will come and then the entirety unravels. We don't think about past breaths we've taken, we focus on the ones we're going to take next. That's survival."

For Ambuya to have said this much, I know for sure she's tired. Not just tired, I correct myself, but weary. It's always been there, the weariness. In the quiet at the kitchen table before I join her for tea in the mornings, in the heavy silences she sits with in the middle of the night when both of us should be asleep. My thoughts return again to Gogo Ropa saying that wars don't end, they just change location.

Before I leave the hospital—a nice private one that's as good as a hotel—Mr. Kingsley Pfupajena does his checks and note-taking, then sits down on the bed.

"So," he huffs, "how are we feeling, all things considered?"

"Fine, I guess. A little washed out." But strangely okay, like I've turned the corner and found myself in a brand-new section of town, where everything is clean and in its place.

"Excellent. Do you have any sense of lethargy, tiredness of any kind?"

"No," I reply.

"Good." He smiles brightly. Under his doctor's coat he's wearing a shirt the color of watermelons and blue pants that really shouldn't go with it, but they do. He smells as if he's walked through a cloud of citrusy men's cologne. Ambuya is wearing a matchy-matchy gray sweatsuit, and while she's fully made up, she looks worn out.

"Ambuya, where is Gogo Ropa?" I ask. "Is she okay?"

It's Mr. Kingsley Pfupajena who answers. "She'll be all right."

"Where is she?" I persist.

I'm surprised when Ambuya replies.

"There's a facility we set up with funding from our diplomatic friends. It's in Vumba. She'll be well taken care of there."

It's when they move Chedu HQ to Ambuya's house to keep an eye on me that I begin crying as if I've never heard of the two-minute rule. If I so much as sigh, it's followed by tears. If I wake in the middle of the night and think of Gogo Ropa's underground bunker, or of Mama or Baba, my heart sinks and tears come until I become fed up with it. After that I mope—recovery, according to Mr. Kingsley Pfupajena—while the gogos plot, plan, and party.

One evening, with the gogos' chatter filtering from

the lounge, I revisit the box of memories. I now recognize papers torn from a notebook as belonging to Gogo Ropa—it's the same scrawly handwriting as the writing on the wall. Most of it is in a kind of code that makes no sense. It reads like Aesop's fables and folktales on TV.

The question highest in my mind is, what happened to Gogo Ropa that left her unable to push things to the back of her life the way the others could? I examine photos searching for clues. I notice it's always Gogo Stella and Ambuya together, without Gogo Ropa, and then, after the war, there are photos with Gogo Tapera and of Mama as a baby. The one thing I can be reasonably sure of was that whatever happened to Gogo Ropa took place between 1976 and 1982. This is nothing and something, and for the first time in days, there's no sign of tears.

Mr. Kingsley Pfupajena comes to sit with me. He makes nice comments about my shoeboxes, especially about the one with him on it. He shuffles through papers I've clipped together and picks up a photo I've taken from the box of memories. He smiles. "Look at Stella."

All the gogos are in that photo except Gogo Tapera. They're young and, with their short hair, could've been mistaken for boys, except they're wearing dresses. They're standing next to a cow by a paddock. Gogo Stella has a long sheaf of dry grass in her mouth and one fist on her hip. Gogo Ropa is holding on to the rope around the cow's neck and squinting into the sun. Ambuya is leaning against the paddock with both arms locked around the top rung. None of them has shoes on, and their feet and legs are dusty. It isn't difficult to tell who's who; though they've aged, there's something about each of them that has remained unchanged.

"The way it is now—feels to me like you've always known each other," I tell Mr. Kingsley Pfupajena. "I sometimes forget that you didn't meet them until the war."

He nods. "We completely depended on each other in those days. We had one objective, and that made us family."

"And you've stayed close all this time," I observe. "Even after the divorce."

"Where would I go? Begin a new life with new people? Not me. War takes so much. You don't give up what's left for any old reason." He sets the photo aside. "Where did you get all these, anyway?"

"From a box of puzzle pieces. I've been trying to make sense of what's in there. It's their life in snippets—here and there I can put it together, but I'm not sure I have the whole truth of it yet. Especially Gogo Ropa's story. Maybe she'll tell me eventually, when she's back from the center."

I'm sitting on my bed leaning against the wall. Mr. Kingsley Pfupajena sits across from me on the stool by the dressing table.

"The war changed many lives," he says. "Hundreds died without the chance to tell their stories. They live on in the details of other people's, and who's to say what is truth? Maybe their families will get a little portion of their dear departed through the recollections of those who knew them. But to be honest, nobody wants to relive the horrors. And you must be wary of those who are too keen to do so—there will be more fiction than fact. Maybe you connected with Ropa's story because she too left home to escape a situation beyond her control?"

"Except she did something worthwhile with her running away. I haven't solved anything," I say.

Mr. Kingsley Pfupajena bursts out laughing. "There is no solving anything in life. Resolving yourself to a situation, maybe. What did you hope to solve?"

I shrug. "I don't know. I need . . . a way to go forward. There was a bridge I walked across every day to get from Point A to Point B, and the bridge got blown up. I guess what I need is a way to mend that bridge."

"The important thing is taking forward action," Mr. Kingsley Pfupajena says. "A bridge cannot mend itself."

I sit up gasping. In my dream I've just hit my head again and fallen into the abyss.

Beyond the curtains, the sun is wondering why it can't see me because it's way past godly hours. I check my phone and see that it's after ten.

My energy is renewed; I'm ready for the next thing. I fell asleep last night wading through the photos and thinking about Gogo Ropa, and I had an idea. I'm excited to talk to Ambuya about it—it's genius and proves to me that the things we go through are not for nothing.

I bound out of bed and grab my gown, but as I open the door I hear a familiar laugh, and I stop cold.

This is not what I want for this day.

SIXTEEN

Tisha comes running and throws herself into my arms. "Kiki, we're here!"

Taren, at the table with Ambuya, doesn't get up. "Hi," she says defiantly.

Tisha is chattering, hanging on to me, and I can't shake her loose. She doesn't get it that I'm not pleased to see her.

"We came on the bus. Old Sourpuss put us on it early this morning but we were happy to be coming. I'm sooooooooo happy to see you, Kiki." She grabs my face and plants a wet kiss in the vicinity of my eye. "Sit down." She pushes me into a chair and sits so close that her overheated little body is making me warm.

I look at Ambuya and she dares me to speak. What her eyes tell me is *This is my house, I do what I please.* She knew they were coming. In fact I suspect she orchestrated it.

"You seem refreshed," Ambuya says.

"I am, thank you," I reply.

"That's good. I wanted to see your sisters before school started again, it's been a while."

I don't say anything as I reach for the teapot and a plate.

"The three of you can have the pleasure of cleaning up, and I can have the pleasure of free labor." Her laugh is diabolical as she takes her cup and walks out of the kitchen. In my mind I kiss my teeth at her.

"I can tell you're not over the moon to see us," Taren says, reaching for another sausage. "but tough. She's our gran too."

"Did you not want to see us?" Tisha asks.

I can't be mad at Tisha—that would be like kicking a kitten. So I smile and say, "It's not that. It's just been difficult for me."

"Us too," Tisha says. She's swinging her legs and drinking milky tea that I'm sure has too much sugar.

"Eat your breakfast," I say.

"Baba went to Namibia for work," Tisha volunteers. "He's been gone a whole week and before that he was always at the office. I wanted to ask him . . ." She stops when Taren kicks her under the table.

This hurts me. Why does Taren think Tisha shouldn't tell me things? I look down and say nothing.

"It's just that . . ." Tisha stops. "I mean, we've hardly seen him since . . ."

"Don't worry about it," I say. "You came to see Ambuya, so see her." With that I leave the table and walk out the front door.

Halfway down the hill I meet Mr. Kingsley Pfupajena. "You're not still keeping an eye on me?" I say.

"Well, good morning to you! How did you sleep?"

I do the morning greeting grumpily because there's no getting around it with older people.

"I see you're not in a good disposition today so I won't bother you. I understand I have the choice of two other young people to join me in my social media escapades, so you don't need to dread me anymore."

"I wasn't dreading you," I say. Damned if I'm going to let Tisha and Taren also have Mr. Kingsley Pfupajena. "Are you doing one now?"

"No, I don't want to bother you, you were on your way to . . . where exactly?"

I turn toward the locked gate of Gogo Ropa's house. For some reason I'm not convinced she's gone.

"I know what you're doing," I say. "I'm not a fan."

"But is it working?" he asks.

"Come on, then." I grab his sleeve and pull him along. "I'm going to pick which video we're doing and I'm styling it too."

It's a disaster. Tisha keeps making funny faces while dancing, and Taren can't get a hang of the steps, though she's usually a good dancer. Even Mr. Kingsley Pfupajena loses his cool and says, "What is this you're doing? Oh nooo!"

The gogos carry on their business as if they can't hear our loud arguing on the verandah.

"Taren, listen to the music!" I urge. "Please! The lyrics tell you what to do."

"I'm doing it."

I have to hold my head in place to keep it from exploding off my neck and rolling down the grassy slope. I want to shake her.

"This is the problem with you!" I yell. "You always do what you want, even when you shouldn't."

"It's just a dance for a stupid video!" she yells.

"Get it right, then!"

She doesn't get it right and we do the best we can. Mr. Kingsley Pfupajena smiles and says, "I'll post it later, the network here is patchy," before escaping into the lounge, probably never to be seen again.

"See?" I say to Taren. "He's not going to upload it."

"So what? Are you his campaign manager? What do you care?"

"I care because before you came we were getting it right and making good videos."

"You're not that great, you know. You just think you are."

At this point Ambuya opens the sliding door and says, "Come in, it's getting late." That's what her voice says. Her face is speaking a different dialect, so we listen to the face and go in.

Cleaning a house is not a problem when it's only two of you. It's a different story when you're four plus a whole commercial enterprise taking place. The gogos drink and eat endlessly and while they do their share, we have no excuse for not doing more. Now with three "maids" to do their bidding, they're really living their best lives. When I tell Taren for the twenty-eleventh time to get off her phone and come wipe the dishes, things get out of hand.

"Tisha can do it," she says.

"It's not Tisha's job, it's yours. Tisha is putting the dishes away."

"Yes, Taren," Tisha pipes up. She's dressing one of her many dolls in new clothes that Gogo Tapera sewed for it. Taren kicks Tisha under the table.

"Stop kicking her and come and do your chore," I say.

"Don't tell me what to do. I'll come when I'm ready."

"Taren, come and do it now. I have to sweep after you guys are done."

"So sweep," she says, attention still on her phone.

"You're being so sassy since you came here, and I've had enough of it!" I march up to Taren and grab her phone.

Her chair topples backward and she jackknifes straight at me, like a kangaroo leaping in slow motion. I don't mean to hit her, but as I move her phone out of reach, she finds herself in the pathway of my arm and next thing we're both on the floor and Taren is wrestling me, getting slaps in any chance she gets.

"Ow! Stop it!" I grunt. "Taren, stop!" I heave up and pin her and she's screaming bloody murder.

Suddenly Ambuya is holding Taren and me like rugby balls under each arm, and I'm amazed at how strong she is. Gogo Tapera comes and takes Taren, who is struggling to get free.

"Kids," Ambuya grumbles as Taren's foot connects

with her shin. "What is wrong with you two nincompoops?" she yells.

The urge to laugh almost overtakes me, but I'm also angry so I let that win.

"Right!" Ambuya sits us down at opposite ends of the kitchen table. Taren's face is thunderous.

"Ambuya, see how she's looking at me," I say. "Why did she even come here?"

"I can be here if I want to! She's not only *your* grandmother."

"Why didn't you stay at your other grandmother's?" I say. "You ruin everything. You don't listen and you're always getting us into trouble."

"You're not that great yourself, Miss Goody Two-Shoes."

"That's why I didn't want to talk to you on the phone. Sometimes I wish I wasn't your sister."

"Well, you're only half my sister, so it's not much to cancel!" she says with tears in her eyes.

At this Tisha gasps, stricken, as though the words have been spoken to her. I'm unmoved. I've been waiting for them.

"I knew it," I say calmly, but my heart is beating fast. "That's why I didn't want to talk to you. You're hateful and I knew you'd say it." I get up to leave.

"You know nothing. Sit." Ambuya doesn't raise her voice, but I hear her loud and clear and sit down.

I can feel the tears coming, and I'm annoyed. I don't want Taren to see that she's made me cry. I take a deep breath.

Tisha hasn't moved and is still clutching her doll in one

hand and the skirt in the other. Tears are streaming from her eyes.

"Tisha," Ambuya says, "do you want to go with Gogo Tapera to the workroom?"

Tisha shakes her head. Gogo Tapera takes a seat.

"I love you kids," Ambuya goes on, "but I'm about ready to send you to your parents. You're being less than a joy and I've had enough stress in my life. My house is not for this." She waves her hand between me and Taren. "This . . . whatever this is that's going on between you."

"You're the one who wanted to see them," I remind her. "It was peaceful before they came."

Ambuya's eyes are slits as they turn on me. "Oh, you suppose we've had peace since you came? Tapera, has it been peaceful these past few days?"

"We had more peaceful days in the bush," Gogo Tapera says.

"Listen up. You'd better tell me what this is about. Otherwise I'm sending you home. I want to enjoy my grandchildren, not be subjected to screaming hooligans every five minutes. Is this how you are with your parents?"

Tisha shakes her head.

"So why do you think you can act this way here?"

None of us want to be the first to speak.

"Taren, what do you have to say for yourself? Chianti is your older sister, you should not be brawling like two hookers in a shebeen."

I wince, but Tisha's expression makes me want to laugh. She's at the zenith of shock.

"Taren, let's hear what you've got to say."

"She's the one who doesn't act like she's our sister, so why should we treat her like it? I can tell Tisha what to do if I want and she doesn't get to override me anymore."

"Is that right?" Ambuya says. Her tone of voice says it's not, and Taren gets the memo. "Tisha? Do you have anything to say?"

Tisha shakes her head.

"What do you think of what Taren has said?"

Tisha sneaks a glance at Taren. "Chianti is the oldest and Taren should listen to her because when Taren doesn't listen we get in trouble and it's boring."

Taren's eyes glare the word *traitor* at Tisha.

"Chianti." Ambuya turns to me.

I have to work through what I'm going to say before I speak. I take a deep breath. The light in the kitchen has gone. Outside the sky is ominous and the trees are dancing wildly.

"Ambuya," I say, "none of this would've happened if Taren had listened to me."

"It's not true!" Taren throws her hands on the table as if she's going to launch it at me. "We would've just gotten in trouble as always. It's your own fault, Kiki, and Mama is the one who screwed everything up. She's the screw-up, not me." She's breathing as if she's run up the hill.

Ambuya gives Taren a sharp look. "That's my daughter you're calling a screw-up. What might you be saying about me, who raised her?"

Taren simmers down, but her chest is heaving.

I'm tired. I don't want to talk anymore. We sit in silence for a minute. Gogo Stella and Mr. Kingsley Pfupajena's muffled voices filter through the living room door, followed by the drilling of the sewing machine and the whistling of the wind.

"Chianti told you not to put the key in the ignition, Taren," Tisha says quietly.

"I didn't ask her to take the blame," Taren says. "Anyway, you're the one who let the brake down."

"I didn't know! I didn't mean to. I only wanted to switch the radio on." Tisha bursts into tears, jumps from the table, and runs out.

SEVENTEEN

"So!" Ambuya says. "This was all an unfortunate accident."

I'm forced to speak. "Baba said if Taren got in trouble one more time he was going to send her to boarding school. I was scared, so I said it was me. When things went from bad to catastrophic, I felt like I'd set myself up and I was angry with everyone."

"You've always got to be the good one," Taren says sullenly. "It makes it worse for me."

"Taren, I try to help you but you think you know better."

"Show a little solidarity once in a while!" Taren shouts.

"Hey!" Ambuya says. Only thing left is for her to blow a referee's whistle.

"I always knew if I wasn't good, something bad would happen," I say.

"That doesn't make sense." Ambuya and Taren speak in stereo.

Once, when I was young, Mama took me to the doctor and outside she met a man. I remember he was scowling and they were arguing. I didn't really catch what they said, but I felt deep inside me that this was happening because of me—that it was my fault, something wrong in me that should be kept secret. For years, impressions of his face, the shape of his eyes and his ears, have floated around my memory when I look in the mirror. I've often wondered if I dreamed it, but now I know it really happened.

Gogo Tapera comes huffing in. "I can't find the little one. She ran into the garden and she's just . . . *poof*!" Gogo Tapera makes a magician's gesture with her hands and suddenly, as if she conjured it, all the rain that heaven can spare comes down in a heavy sheet of liquid metal.

Tisha is nowhere. Mr. Kingsley Pfupajena checks to see if the cameras captured where she went. Seconds before the rain, there's Tisha running out of Ambuya's gate, and then it's obscured by the downpour.

"I don't believe this." Ambuya grabs her hair in both hands. "She'd better have the sense to turn around and come back in."

Ambuya doesn't know Tisha well, obviously. When she gets herself into a state, she's that fly that dies on the windowsill staring at freedom even though you've opened every window. She could easily end up lost in the bush, and in this rain, who's able to see anything?

Ambuya, the gogos, and Mr. Kingsley Pfupajena seem to be in no rush, putting on rain gear in a leisurely manner and hunting for flashlights and car keys. I want to yell at them to hurry. With the passing seconds I'm more convinced that Tisha is in acute danger of death. I fight the breathlessness and keep my thoughts and dysfunction to myself.

The rain outside sounds like the end of the world.

"Hey!" Taren says in such a forceful voice that I jump.

"What?"

"Snap out of it," Taren says. "You're already in disaster-has-fallen mode. She's going to be fine. They've probably found her by now." Taren wants to believe the words she's saying, but she's scared too.

"Walking to your room muttering about *shouldn't have done this*, *shouldn't have done that* . . . shoulda woulda coulda, my guy, it doesn't matter, things are how they are."

I want to laugh. Despite it being so messed up, unexpectedly, life seems normal. This is classic Taren: nothing's a trainwreck, even if it is. I need that level of optimism in my life.

"What's wrong with you, anyway?" she asks. "You've always been a worrywart but you're on another level since Mama's announcement. You'd better get okay. You know life's a bitch, right? Even when this crap with Mama and

Baba is sorted, it's going to be something else, so if you break now you're done for."

I'm exhausted, but I must older-sister up and take our minds off the thing we can't do anything about. I turn to my shoeboxes. "What do you think?"

"It's Tisha and me!" she says with a smile. "I love it. And these ones. Oh," she says as she comes to the one of Mama, "this box not so much. What's up with you, anyway? Ambuya told us you haven't been well. Is it anxiety?"

"It's complicated," I say.

"I thought you were better. Ambuya said so."

"I am, I guess."

"Is it because we came? Do you hate us that much?"

"I don't hate you," I say.

"You shouldn't have taken the blame for the car. I might've been sent to boarding school in the middle of nowhere, but who cares?"

"I care," I say. "I didn't want you to go. You'd hate it. Those schools are strict."

"So what? At least Mama wouldn't have felt the need to say what she said."

"She would've said it another time. She knew it was true and didn't want to lie anymore. Maybe that's why Mama had become impossible. Telling the secret set her free. Baba is a decent man. I guess the guilt about never telling him the truth had become too much."

"Maybe," Taren says. "Maybe it's okay. In any case, it's taught me a lesson."

"What lesson?" I ask.

“That the things I do affect everyone and it’s not just me getting into trouble.” She looks down at her hands clasped in her lap.

“I didn’t want you to go to boarding school. I would’ve missed you,” I say. “I didn’t take the blame for your sake—I was afraid of what home would be like without you. Those guys are hard work, and I can’t do it on my own.”

“Yeah, ’cause Tisha’s oblivious. At Ambuya Minana’s I kept wishing you were there. She really loves you.” She rolls her eyes. “So ironic.”

I laugh. “Yeah, she thinks I’m wonderful. Shame.” Taren laughs.

We hear the door open and the gogos’ voices. We don’t dawdle.

They didn’t find her. It’s not raining so viciously anymore, but they’re beat.

“We looked everywhere,” Ambuya says.

My heart sinks.

“We can only hope she’s had the common sense to find shelter.”

They’re dripping water all over the hallway floor. Taren hurries to get a mop, and I help them off with their rain gear. My arms and legs are carrying lead weights and I’m trying not to imagine the worst, but it’s hard. In my head Mama is wailing about how her best child got buried in a mudslide, Baba gives up on us and turns to alcohol, and Taren and I forever drown in guilt. And poor sweet silly Tisha gets discovered many years later when they’re digging out foundations for a new housing development.

I want to yell at Ambuya to get back out there and find Tisha, but I hold my tongue. Why have they returned if they haven't found her?

Ambuya peers at me as she fluffs out her hair. "Chianti, are you okay?"

"I'm fine, Ambuya," I say quickly.

"Ambuya, shall I make tea? I'll make tea," Taren says decisively. "Kiki will help me."

She grabs me and pulls me into the kitchen and pushes me into a chair.

"Whatever you were about to say is just going to make them mad," Taren hisses. "They know what they're doing." But I hear the muttered "I hope!" as she turns away.

"Taren," Gogo Tapera calls out, "bring us glasses, dear."

"Take the short fat ones," I tell her. It's half-past whisky o'clock. I'm more than familiar with the drill.

Taren bustles about, pulling a chair up to reach the shelf. She gets out a tray, and I tell her to put ice cubes in a bowl and take a jug of water.

It's a subdued whisky party. Taren and I sit in the kitchen drinking tea, not saying much. I put a lot of sugar in mine, like Ambuya has been doing, and gradually I feel better.

"Maybe I need a shot of whisky," I say to Taren.

She laughs. "Please! I'm sure it would just about kill you. You're not the type."

"How do you know?" I challenge her.

As she's about to answer, we hear a commotion coming

from the hallway. It's Mr. Kingsley Pfupajena with a bundle of towels in his arms.

"Right by my door," he says. "Behind the potted palm. Curled up and crying like a lost puppy."

Tisha. Thank God.

"Oh, thank you, Jesus!" Gogo Stella holds her arms up and does a little dance.

Ambuya takes Tisha from Mr. Kingsley Pfupajena. "Oh, you silly thing," she says, "look at you. Why did you run away like that?"

Tisha sniffs. Taren and I both roll our eyes, but the weight of the sky on our heads has been lifted. Even the tiredness leaves me, and I suddenly have strength.

"Let me take her, Ambuya," I say. I carry her on my back. Tisha lays her head on my shoulders.

Behind us we hear the whisky party get a bit louder. The gogos sing about Mr. Kingsley Pfupajena being a hero.

Tisha is barely awake through her bath. Taren and I scold her while scrubbing with the soapy washcloth.

"Don't ever do that again," I say in my strictest voice.

"Yes," Taren chimes. "You aged us ten years tonight! What did you do that for?"

We stop when tears make tracks over Tisha's wet face.

"Okay, okay," I say, "at least, you're safe."

"I didn't know it would rain so hard and I got confused. I couldn't see where I was going. Everyone was being so mean and I just wanted to get away."

Ambuya comes to rub Vicks all over Tisha's chest and

back and under her feet. She also gives her a concoction that I suspect has a dash of whisky, but Ambuya says it's medicine and to mind our own business, are we doctors?

We sleep in my bed. Tisha is in the middle breathing on my neck, but I don't mind. Even though I haven't wanted them here, I know now that I've needed them.

EIGHTEEN

It's late when I wake up and make my way to the kitchen. I hear Taren's voice from the hallway.

"What happened to your husband, Gogo Stella?"

"I killed him."

Taren gasps.

I hear Gogo Stella cackle. "Oh, you should see your face. No child, I didn't kill him. I divorced him. I love him very much, but he was troublesome. I ran out of patience with his behavior. Marriage didn't suit him so I set him free."

"And you, Gogo Tapera?"

"I need peace and quiet, and all the men in my life talk too much. When I meet a peaceful man maybe I'll think about it."

"About getting married? At your age, Gogo?"

"Is there a cutoff age?"

"No, I mean . . ."

"There's no timetable to life. That's half the trouble

with the world—people work according to a schedule that others have set. That's why there are so many unhappy people. I'm always telling my daughter, first be happy, then do the rest. It's not a race."

When I enter the kitchen, the only person missing is Mr. Kingsley Pfupajena. Tisha is in Gogo Tapera's lap being babied and soaking it up. Everyone has a cup of tea, and there's a map taking up most of the table.

"Good morning, Ambuya. Good morning, Gogos. How did you sleep?"

In response there's a chorus of "good mornings" and "we slept well if you slept well."

"I slept well," I say, and this is not a lie. It was nice to have my sisters close.

"We're talking about our plan of action," Ambuya says, pulling out a chair for me. "We've advanced money to our vendors so we'll get clothing bales next week.'"

"Why not buy the bales yourselves?" I ask.

"Where's the fun in that? Anyway, we just want the good stuff. And things have to appear normal so the robbers don't catch on that it's a trap."

"We're finalizing a plan to teach those thugs a lesson," adds Gogo Tapera. "They won't see us coming."

"See here . . ." Gogo Tapera leans forward and traces a line on the map. I watch her finger, visualizing trees and bushes. "This is a route I took often at the onset of the war when I carried supplies and messages back and forth across enemy lines. I should've died or been captured many times, but I would get warning."

"You were a spy!" Taren gasps.

"Of a kind," Gogo Tapera says. "I was so daring in those days. The last run I made was with medical supplies. Mr. Kingsley Pfupajena worked as a hospital orderly and had access to things needed by the fighters; he would gather what he could and I would make a run. It was risky, and on that last run, the fear wouldn't leave my heart. I went anyway. Ropa was sent to warn me that around the hill, in the next village, there was an ambush waiting and I should make my escape."

"Who is Gogo Ropa?" Tisha asks.

I'm not surprised that she doesn't remember Gogo Ropa, who never featured much during our brief visits. It's only since I came to stay that all the gogos have become a part of my life.

"She's our sister," Ambuya says. "In English you would call her a cousin. Our fathers were brothers—mine, Gogo Stella's, and Gogo Ropa's."

"I met Ropa and we became bond sisters," adds Gogo Tapera. "We returned to Chimoio base camp together, but I didn't stay long. I was sent on another assignment, and we met again two years later in Tanzania."

"Tanzania?"

"Yes, we were sent for further training there. Both of us were good at stealth tactics and evasion. I also trained in mechanics. Anyway, let's focus on the operation at hand."

"Ahh, I want to hear more stories about being spies in the war!" Taren complains.

"Another day," Ambuya says.

“Actually,” Gogo Stella chimes in, “you can probably get firsthand experience if we settle on a good plan.”

“Stella, no!” says Ambuya. “That’s asking for disaster. We’ve managed so far without reporting ourselves to Tamara. How about we keep the peace?”

“We were barely children ourselves,” Gogo Stella replies.

I speak up. “I have an idea.”

I haven’t been able to stop thinking about Gogo Ropa sitting with me in the forest. I see her eyes staring at me through her camouflage. Hokoyo Chipokouyo—Beware the Ghost.

“But if we do it, you have to let us come along,” I say.

Ambuya readily agrees, probably because she doesn’t imagine there’s any danger of my idea being good.

“Let’s hear it,” Gogo Tapera says.

NINETEEN

We are doing my idea! Even Ambuya can't deny that it's genius. The whole thing about Gogo Ropa had gotten me thinking—camouflage, ghosts, and wartime movements.

When we tell Mr. Kingsley Pfupajena my plan, he laughs and laughs. He knows exactly where to plant a story of "mysterious" happenings near the border where the robbers will cross to ambush the smugglers.

"We won't get into Heaven," Tisha says with a worried frown.

"Then you should stay behind," Taren says.

"Kiki, don't you want to get into Heaven?" Tisha asks me plaintively.

"Of course, but God will understand. We're not stealing and we're not breaking a law. The government can't make up their minds—one day it's not allowed, another day it is. Let them decide! Meanwhile, people need to keep living and affording clothes."

"Okay, okay," Taren jumps in. "Do you want to give a sermon about economics or are we going to practice? Time is opportunity, guys. If Gogo Stella comes to check on us and we haven't hit one bullseye, she says we don't get to go."

We want to go and so we get down to practicing.

The afternoon flies by, and before you can say gangbusters it's early evening. Mr. Kingsley Pfupajena is sitting in the living room, laughing. We're all here except for Ambuya. In the tree by the verandah, there's a bird cooing about night coming. It's not the trill of the gaudy birds from daylight hours. They seem almost boring now—not as loud or sharply sonic, just normal.

"I did one better than simply plant a story. I prophesied." Mr. Kingsley Pfupajena finally calms down enough to continue. "I said, I dreamed that I saw a great lion roaring at the mouth of Mutupo Cave, and then a shadow fell upon the plain. This disturbed me greatly in my spirit, I said. The ancestors are not happy. The balance of things in Gandanga Plain has been disturbed."

"What ancestors?" Tisha asks. She's curled up in an armchair holding a cup of tea like an adult at an afternoon salon.

"It doesn't matter, my dear. The minute you talk about making ancestors angry, people don't ask questions," Mr. Kingsley Pfupajena replies. "Those young thugs will get the message. But they imagine they're invincible with their black magic charms from the old man."

"What old man?" I ask.

"There is an old man that everyone refers to as Old Man. He is feared around here for his potions and spells."

"You're not afraid?" Tisha asks with wide eyes.

"I fear only God," Mr. Kingsley Pfupajena says. "And anyway, we don't need magic. We have this." He points to his head. "Ever heard of Tsuro and Gudo?"

We nod.

"Well, as you know, Tsuro could beat any of the animals, no matter how large, small, tall, slow, fast, clever. He was just a hare, but he was cunning."

"Did he die in the war?" Tisha asks.

Mr. Kingsley Pfupajena roars with laughter.

"Don't laugh at the child," Gogo Tapera says. She and Gogo Stella are busy sewing leaves and attaching twigs to a large piece of netting. "Don't mind him," she says to Tisha. "Tsuro can never die. Only the storyteller dies. Tsuro is a legend."

Ambuya comes in with a huge bag. "Pulleys, ropes, speakers, walkie-talkies, pebbles. Tapera, Gentleman will deliver the stuff you need. He says he'll configure it with as many variations as possible, but if those mambaras use a car that doesn't have central locking then we have to be ready with a backup plan. And he's good to go for cleanup after."

Tisha laughs out loud. "Gentleman? Is that his name, Ambuya? I mean, really?"

"Why wouldn't it be?" Ambuya asks.

"He is in fact a real gentleman," Gogo Tapera says, "truly a fine young man."

"So was he born with Gentleman as his name? Or is he a gentleman and was given that nickname?"

"It doesn't matter," Gogo Stella says. "It works, just as this plan is going to work."

For a moment I'm scared. What if it only seemed great in my mind?

"Don't frown, Kiki," Ambuya says. "Otherwise I will believe you have no faith in your idea."

"To be honest, Ambuya, I hadn't thought about it that hard and I'm not sure why you agreed to it."

"It's simple and it's fun. I may be a serious person, but don't ever threaten me with a good time." Ambuya cackles.

"It's genius," Gogo Tapera says.

I'm growing to fill every inch of my body. I might keep growing until I burst.

"Devious," Mr. Kingsley Pfupajena says and laughs again. He rubs his palms together. "I can't wait."

"Ha!" Taren jumps up. "I knew there was a bad girl in there." She high-fives me.

"Tisha, are you going to keep it together? Are you going to be cool?" I ask.

Tisha puts her cup down on the coffee table, folds her arms across her chest. "Ice cool," she says. We all laugh and I almost call out for whisky.

We're in position. The sky is overcast. There is no light from the moon and no stars. Ambuya said it was a good sign for our mission. There's faint thunder and the wind is gusting on and off.

Ambuya and the gogos have drilled us on the plan. We've come out here a couple of nights and once in daylight to understand the lay of the land. I've been teamed up with Tisha, who sulked the first night but hasn't fidgeted or spoken since we arrived, hidden behind a cluster of rocks. Taren is in complete camouflage a ways across from us. Ambuya, the gogos, and Mr. Kingsley Pfupajena have kept their hideaways secret.

"In case you're captured and tortured, you won't be able to give up our positions to the enemy," Gogo Stella said. I don't think she was serious, but she might've been, and not being able to tell worries me. It keeps me alert.

Our eyes have adjusted to the dark now. Before we left, Ambuya and Gogo Stella started their foot-stomping war song and made us join in, answering to their call of "Boots on the ground for the revolution!" I could see why they did it; it made me want to run out and be fierce.

I hear the first trill of the nightjar. Then again. From nearby, there's a response. Then the almost-bark of a night heron. We come to attention and wait. When we hear voices and see a flash of white, Tisha draws her catapult and lets loose the first stone.

There's a muted "*Eyiii!*" Then heavy thuds, followed by "Ko chii, Teki?"

"Something hit me!" Teki responds. I sense him peering in our direction.

"Haaaa, stop being . . . *eyii!*"

Taren's stone finds a target. There's another thud as they drop the bale of goods they were carrying.

Beside me Tisha loads another stone. I draw mine and let it fly. Then it's chaos.

Stones are raining onto the pathway and the five robbers are jumping around, ducking, crying out and trying to take cover. I know Mr. Kingsley Pfupajena's club has found a mark when I hear a *thunk* and a loud howl. I almost laugh—Mr. Kingsley Pfupajena has a short club with a clear elastic cord, which he throws, and it bounces back.

"Heyi, mhani!"

I see everything in the dim light. One of the robbers is rubbing his head. Another switches on a flashlight.

"Heyi! What was that?" They scramble, but we're already moving away, melting into shadows. We hear the men thrashing about in the bushes, but we're safe now behind a large tree. Silently we climb up the lowest branches and sit as still as the stones around us.

"Kaitano! I told you. I told you what that war veteran said."

"Ha, there's nothing like that! It's people being mischievous."

"Where? Where are the people this late at night?"

The disbeliever thrashes around in the bushes with a machete. The reality of how dangerous our mission is hits me, and I begin to question Ambuya's judgment.

"Kinso, let's go. There's no time to play hide-and-seek with ghosts."

Kinso the disbeliever hefts up his load with his partner,

and they make their way to their pickup truck. Gogo Tapera is waiting for them there with a nice surprise.

We wait until we hear the trill. Once, twice, and then the response. *Move out.*

We take the long route Gogo Stella marked for us with lengths of string hidden in leaves. We arrive at the spot where Gogo Tapera moved the robbers' truck, which she has left parked with the lights on.

"That's not where I parked," one robber is saying. We can see them clearly in the headlights. Three of them are young, but the other two are hulking and scary, and one has a scar across his face. "I locked the doors! You all heard it. And we parked by the tree. How did the truck move here?"

"He's not wrong—the truck wasn't here and I heard him lock it," Scarface replies. His voice sounds like he has sand in his throat. I get goosebumps and move a little farther away. Tisha is in silent agreement.

"Boys, we have to go. Load the merchandise and let's get out of here." They get busy loading two huge bales, then jump in and get ready to leave.

The engine coughs and dies. The lights go out. There's the clicking of locks, a split second of silence, and the netting with leaves and twigs falls onto the truck and covers the cab completely.

Ambuya and Gogo Tapera appear on either side and pull straps, securing it tight. There's muffled shouting from within. Mr. Kingsley Pfupajena and the gogos rock the truck once, violently, then make as much noise as possible with the canopy of leaves and twigs. They heft the bulky bales onto the tailgate of the truck and drop them on the ground before melting into the vegetation around them.

There's thumping and banging from inside the truck, and it rocks. I wish I could see the robbers' faces. I'm sure life isn't so great for them right about now.

For a moment it's dead quiet.

A cacophony of sound rings out across the forest—a resounding, rhythmic gong with weird forest noises and the cry of hyenas: "Whooooo we! Whooooo we!"

The hairs on my body rise to attention, even though I'm aware that it's Gogo Tapera's speaker system doing its thing.

The net is lifted abruptly, and a piercing beam of light from the trees illuminates the truck. The sounds stop, and in the abrupt lull, the robbers flinch from the brightness and try to open the doors.

Their instinct to run seems to dissolve when they see no one and nothing but the bales of goods on the ground. This scares them more than anything because what's waiting for them outside might not be an encounter geared toward their well-being. The driver is trying to start the truck but there's only a click as the key turns over.

Out of nowhere, Mr. Kingsley Pfupajena's club comes flying through the air and sharply raps the windshield. We hear muffled screaming.

Next to me, Tisha giggles quietly. I want to laugh too, but I don't trust myself to stop, so I hold it in.

The locks on the doors click open, and I have to clamp my hands over my mouth as the robbers rush to lock the doors again themselves. I'm hot and stressed from trying to hold in the laughter.

A stone hits the body of the car and that's our cue. One each, and then all together with the gogos and Mr. Kingsley Pfupajena. The netting comes down again; the straps are secured. Mr. Kingsley Pfupajena, Ambuya, and the gogos silently shift the bales into the trees and camouflage them. We move to the agreed point and watch as the bales become part of the forest.

Mr. Kingsley Pfupajena hustles us away to our own car, which is more than a short jog through unchartered bush. Behind us, we hear the eerie noises start up again.

We pile into Gogo Tapera's Defender and chatter excitedly, but Mr. Kingsley Pfupajena makes us hush and be still.

"Not now," he says. "We're in the field. The mission is only over when every operative is accounted for." We quiet the bubbling inside us.

Even though Gentleman is coming to fetch the bales and release the smugglers tied up by the robbers, Ambuya and the gogos have stayed behind to make sure they've left no evidence. It seems hours before they join us. They pile in and sit silently while Mr. Kingsley Pfupajena rolls the car down the small incline. He doesn't start the engine or switch the lights on until the car comes to a stop by the paved road.

The first roar of laughter jerks Tisha awake. The gogos and Mr. Kingsley Pfupajena laugh until tears stream from their eyes, slapping each other's backs, clasping hands, and recounting the looks on the robbers' faces.

"Today those boys saw fire! Who did they think they were messing with?" Ambuya says, wiping her eyes and blowing her nose in a tissue.

"Ambuya," Taren says, leaning over the seat, "that was so exciting and scary. I want to keep doing missions with you and the gogos. Is this what it was like during the war?"

They laugh.

"If only war had been such an adventure," Gogo Stella says when she stops cackling. "Child, in war, nothing seems real, not even yourself. War is a red-hot thing you agree to hold because you have no idea of pain. No," she says, "it was not like this during the war."

No one says a thing until we arrive home.

TWENTY

"Uh-oh," Ambuya says under her breath as we pull up to the gate. It's almost four o'clock in the morning.

Gogo Stella huffs out a breath. "You can say that again."

Mama's car is parked in the driveway of Ambuya's house.

"She might be asleep," Mr. Kingsley Pfupajena says.

But the door opens and Mama is standing in the entrance with her arms crossed.

Baba comes up behind her, and my heart jumps through the windshield. Since Tisha and Taren arrived, I've barely thought about him and Mama. Now here they are before the sun is up, and a fight is happening across Mama's face, which none of us want to be here for.

"Mama! What could you be thinking? Where are you coming from with the children at this hour?" Mama is fuming, especially when she sees our faces covered in camouflage paint. "What is this?" She smears her fingers across Tisha's cheek.

Tisha scowls, and Mama gives her a talking eye. When Tisha's been sleeping she's a different animal. She slouches and garummphs into the house.

"Hello, Tamara. What are you doing here?" Ambuya says, as if addressing delegates at a conference.

"Mama, what are the kids doing out and dressed in this manner so late at night?"

"Come inside," says Ambuya, so we all troop into the living room and find seats. Taren and I are squashed together in one of the armchairs; it's safer. I'm expecting to be told to go to bed, but no one says it.

We take the break in the conversation to tell Mama and Baba hello and how are they, we are fine if they are fine. I don't look at them. Conflict and time apart have made them strangers—they don't feel like home anymore.

Baba greets everyone with more than average respect. He is an in-law and even if he is mad, he needs to mind his manners. Baba is not the kind of person to shoot flames anyway.

"Drink?" Gogo Tapera asks. Baba respectfully says no, and Mama gives Gogo Tapera a dirty look.

"Hehedeee! Tamara!" Gogo Tapera cackles. "Who are you giving that stink-eye? You think you're a big enough woman to take me on? You better fix your face."

Mama takes in the gogos and Mr. Kingsley Pfupajena and gets the message that even if she's in the right, she is greatly outnumbered.

"Tamara," Ambuya says, "I'm happy you've finally come for your children. You too, Tinashe. It took you long enough."

Ambuya really knows how to defuse a bomb. Mama immediately calms down. I can tell she's thinking more clearly about where all this started.

"Now," Ambuya continues, "I won't tell you off in front of your children, but what I will say is you need to watch your tone when speaking to me. I'm not one of your band members."

I don't need to see Mama's face to know she is percolating inside. Baba will have his eyes examining his hands, wherever he's placed them.

Gogo Tapera comes in with their "adult beverage" and cups of sweet milky tea for Taren and me. She winks at us before sitting back between Gogo Stella and Mr. Kingsley Pfupajena.

"The girls are fine," Ambuya says. "They are happy, healthy, and well cared for, which is more than I can say about Chianti when she first showed up here."

Ambuya's reprimand is a direct hit. For a second I sympathize with Mama. I'm not used to seeing her this way. I take a quick peek at Baba, and my heart twists into a knot. My mind is blank. I'm scared of what he's come to say.

"Tinashe," Ambuya continues, "you too have been negligent and I have words for you, but we'll talk later. The kids are exhausted and so are we all."

With that, she gets up and heads to her room. We're fast on her heels, not wanting to get caught on the tail end and deal with Mama and Baba on our own. The gogos and Mr. Kingsley Pfupajena help us by taking their time getting up and making their way out.

*

When we finally wake it's long after morning. We don't get out of bed immediately. Tisha is the first to sit up.

"Listen," she says, "whatever they say, we don't want to be split up again and you guys have to say so. If they don't want to be married anymore, that's their choice. We should have a choice to stay sisters in the same house, going to the same grannies together. We're kids and it's not our fault they had us and so they shouldn't punish us for their mistakes."

Taren jumps in fast. "She's not saying you're a mistake, Kiki."

"You don't have to defend Tisha if she says something wrong. I don't like it—almost as if you're protecting her from me."

"It's not that," Taren says.

"Then what is it?"

"I don't know . . . I'm just scared someone is going to say the wrong thing. I don't want anyone to be angry because then things get crappy and I hate everything and everyone and it's too much." Taren bursts into tears.

I get a tissue from the box by the bed and give it to her. "We're badass chicks who fight thug-robbers," I say. "Mama and Baba aren't half as scary. We can handle them."

Taren wipes her eyes and blows her nose.

"If they try to separate us, we'll run away," Tisha says.

I don't try to reason it out. I just say, "Yes, we will."

We take our time going to the kitchen. I'm surprised Mama hasn't come to check on us. I get another surprise when we walk into the living room and I'm greeted by shouts of "Happy birthday, Kiki!"

Sixteen years of my life sit me down to explain how I could've forgotten my own birthday. Tisha and Taren both gasp; they'd forgotten too.

Baba comes forward holding a cake. He's smiling as if the past few weeks didn't happen, as if no one has crashed a car or said killing words.

"Happy birthday, Chianti. You're sixteen now."

I smile, but only with my lips. The rest of me is sifting through the gift horse's mouth.

Everyone sings "Happy Birthday," and I feel self-conscious. I don't want to be the center of attention. But I'm glad they didn't let the day I turn sixteen slip away in the chaos of this new life we've been living.

I blow out the candles and cut the cake. Mama and Baba hug me, but I don't hug them back. I'm still mad. When Ambuya, the gogos, and Mr. Kingsley Pfupajena give me hugs, I'm happy and laugh as they make their jokes.

I try my best to avoid finding myself alone with Mama or Baba. We didn't part well and if we look each other in the eye, the truth of that might breach the good vibes that have claimed this day.

"I have to leave and get the preparations going," Mr. Kingsley Pfupajena says. "Tinashe, you're my sous chef, so make your way to my place in about an hour. You're in charge of setup too, so don't be late." With that he bustles out.

"What is he going to do, Ambuya?" I ask.

"Oh, he's going to cook a great feast for your birthday. He's been planning it for a while, since . . ." Ambuya trails off. I'm guessing it's since he probably saw my date of birth in the hospital paperwork. Well, I'm not going to talk about hospitals if Ambuya isn't.

"Let's sit," Ambuya says, indicating the cluttered dining room table. We've never used it before. There are cups, a teapot, and plates with bits of cake and crumbs strewn everywhere. "Right—we're going to have a family meeting." Ambuya's dressed in a turquoise T-shirt with *#FOMO* spelled out in bold black lettering, black leggings, and Tommy canvas shoes, but her attitude reads pantsuit with heels. The Gogos are wearing their favorite colorful boubous and dangly earrings.

"Everyone is going to say what they want to say," Ambuya continues, "calmly and with respect. If anyone is out of order, Gogo Stella will escort them to a place where they can compose themselves before returning."

I smile at Gogo Stella, picturing her as the bouncer of the meeting, but she stays serious and doesn't smile at anyone.

"Who wants to go first?" Ambuya asks, her pointed gaze suggesting Mama.

Mama clears her throat. "Chianti, I'm sorry. Taren, Tisha, Tinashe . . . I wronged all of you. And worse, I left and didn't take care of my family."

She stops to take a breath.

"I made a gigantic mess and didn't hang around to clean it up. I see now that I've done this most of my life, and none of you deserved to be treated like that. I could say I didn't have the same upbringing as other kids, but that would be putting blame on people who've actually been a blessing to me. Who wouldn't want a group of fierce, fun mothers who allowed me to be myself? I often wished for more guidance because I never seemed to make the right choices. I've had a long time to think about this and maybe that's why I needed to be selfish and go away. Doesn't make it right—I should've done better. And I'm going to try."

"We spoiled you," Gogo Stella says roundly. "We should've been more strict."

"You were the worst offender, Mama Stella," Mama says. "You're probably the most to blame."

"What?!" Gogo Stella is taken aback, but she laughs. "Yes, I'm guilty."

"I don't want any more secrets," Mama continues. "It was eating me up, and the nicer your father was to me, the worse I felt. I guess that's why the fights were happening. Chianti . . ."

She takes my hand. My heart is beating fast.

"When I was expecting you, I chose not to stay with your biological father. I knew he wouldn't be good to us. I thought I was being responsible and a good mother by choosing a better man to raise you. I was proud of myself—I thought I'd made such a grown-up decision. It was the right decision, but the way I did it was wrong. I should've been honest with your dad. I picked him because he was steady and reliable and kind."

Baba is staring at the table as if his bonus check is

stuck to it. Shame—Mama didn't even say she fell in love with him.

"When I saw how good he was and how much he loved you, I began to see how wrong I'd been. And that never went away. It grew and grew until it became unbearable. I couldn't tell the truth. I didn't want to lose everything. But I was ruining it and I didn't know what to do. I lost control of the whole thing and became impossible."

No one says anything. We sit there trying to hear Mama's words, waiting for our hearts to decide if they are enough.

Mama clears her throat. "I've spoken to your dad." She throws a glance at him, but he doesn't raise his head. "And if you want to meet your biological—"

"No!" Both Tisha and Taren speak up. Ambuya gives them a look.

"I mean, no," Tisha says more quietly. 'We don't want any new dads around here."

"It's not your turn, Tisha, and your mother wasn't talking to you, so hush," Ambuya says.

Tisha is mutinous, but a glance from Gogo Stella makes her settle down.

Mama repeats, "If you want . . ."

"No," I say. "No new dads." I glance at Baba and he's looking at me. I turn away. I'm still mad that he never called, that he was just *typing* and never pressed Send.

Mama heaves a sigh and says, "Okay."

Tisha raises her hand. "I want to go next, Ambuya. You said everyone can have a turn, you didn't give us numbers."

"Okay, Tisha. Tamara, are you done?"

Mama nods.

"Stella, Tapera, anything to add to what Tamara has said?"

They both shake their heads.

"Go ahead, Tisha."

"I want to say it wasn't Chianti's fault about the car, but she's the one who got the worst punishment. It wasn't fair. And Mama, it wasn't fair that Baba left us at the other ambuya's and that Kiki had to come here by herself. She could've been kidnapped. Me and Taren, we were so scared. Kiki wouldn't answer our calls. It was bad and we don't want to do it again, so if Kiki goes anywhere, we're going too, and we'll be our own family, because you haven't been making this one work."

"I agree with Tisha," Taren pipes up. "The accident with the car was my fault and I think you knew it. Kiki is always responsible and Mukoma Ben taught her how to properly start the car and put it in park and stuff."

Baba sighs deeply and finally lifts his head. "I shouldn't have overreacted. I was already so angry."

He doesn't look at Mama but I know it was about the both of them.

"We haven't been the best people for a while now, and we haven't done our best as parents. I wasn't angry with you, and I'm not upset with you. Chianti, you're a wonderful daughter. Thoughtful, kind, responsible. We can always depend on you to do your best. We shouldn't have put you through this. I needed room to let the situation sink in, but there was a crisis at work, I couldn't deal with both, my head was spinning . . . It wasn't so much the fact I'm not your biological father as the enormity of the lie, for so long, and what it might mean. But you're my kid. I raised you. You don't just wake up one day and your child isn't yours anymore! That doesn't make sense."

I'm so relieved, I'm dizzy. I have to remember to breathe. I repeat what he said in my head so I can confirm I heard what I heard and understood it. I don't even hear what he says to Tisha and Taren.

"What does it mean?" I blurt out. "Does it mean we're going to stay together? Is that what you're saying?"

Baba glances at Mama before he speaks. "It means . . . it means we're going to try and see how it goes."

"And if it doesn't work?" I don't want maybes. That would mean staying ready for anything, and I'm tired.

"We are going to try and make it work," Baba says again.

"Trying isn't good enough!" Taren bangs her fists on the table. "You have to decide you want it to work and *make* it work. We're not coming home if you're only going to *try*. Ambuya and the gogos aren't going to split up and split us up because they're *trying*."

"Yeah," Tisha says. "Mr. Kingsley Pfupajena can be our granddad. Baba, you and Mama can visit. And if we have to go to Ambuya Minana, the three of us go together or Taren and I won't go." She folds her arms across her chest.

Gogo Stella laughs. "Okay, okay, steady."

Gogo Tapera pulls Tisha close and gives her a hug. "So much like your mother at her age." She smiles. "I remember,

Tamara, you once declared that if anyone made you and Dorothy eat more bologna sandwiches you were going on a hunger strike because why couldn't we accept that you disliked them?" Both gogos chuckle.

"Who doesn't enjoy bologna?" Ambuya says. "It's cheap and tasty."

"I still detest it," Mama says.

"You don't know what's good," Gogo Tapera says.

After that there's silence. A ceasefire.

"Right," Ambuya says. "No one has to decide anything this minute. Everyone has enough to think about. We're going to the party at four thirty. Tinashe and Tamara, you will stay here for the next couple of days and manage your children. I'm moving in with Tapera."

Gogo Stella steps in. "Girls, come with me and Gogo Tapera. We have special birthday clothes for you. Tamara, come and pick out an outfit, and Tinashe, Mr. Kingsley Pfupajena will find something appropriate for you to wear at his place."

I love Gogo Stella. Let Mama and Baba start their *trying* right this minute and maybe, when we get back, they will have decided if they're going to *do*, not just try.

TWENTY-ONE

At Gogo Stella's house, it's excitement, noise, energy. Ambuya puts on jazzy music as if we're in a swanky cafe in New Orleans. She even takes out a slim cigarette and reclines in one of Gogo Stella's sofas to light up.

"Ambuya, you smoke?"

"Now and again," she says, blowing out a perfect ring. "When I'm stressed."

"Can I try?" Taren asks with bright eyes.

Ambuya laughs. "No. It's an unhealthy habit. Go put on your dress." She closes her eyes and hums along to the music.

Tisha walks in with a huge smile and does a twirl. "Look!" she says, holding her arms out. The gogos have put her in layers and layers of princessy fabric. It's floating around, and her hair is a fluffy afro-puff. I'm surprised she let anyone touch her tender head. Maybe excitement made her forget about pain.

"Wow, Tisha!" Taren jumps up. "Me next," she says and dashes from the room.

"Let me see you." Ambuya beckons Tisha closer, but Tisha hangs back.

"Why don't I wait till you're done smoking?" she says.

Ambuya laughs and winks. "There's a future for you in diplomacy, kid. Okay, go on, both of you." We go on and leave her to her now-and-again smoking.

While Gogo Stella is pinning my hair into buns and swirls, I can't help thinking of Gogo Ropa. It's strange, but I miss her. I wonder what she would say about everything that's happened.

Love is just a word until it's put into action, she told me.

I watch Gogo Tapera fixing a seam that Taren has burst on her silver rainbow tassel dress from shimmying too much. My dress is a black sequined shift with gold daisies. It has a sleeveless bodice and a short shimmering cape that's like liquid gold. Ambuya has given me a pair of flat gold sandals with sparkly jewels. "You get the special ones. You're the birthday girl."

When I recall the events of the last few weeks, I think surely I should be older; I've lived a whole life since we went to sit in the car because Mama and Baba were fighting.

We're admiring ourselves in the full-length mirror in the living room when I hear the birds.

"Taren," I say, "come with me."

"Where?" she asks, but she doesn't pull her hand away.

"I'm coming too," Tisha says and latches on to my other hand.

We go out into the yard. There's a burst of flowering bushes, clinging vines, jasmine-scented grass, bougainvillea archways and bold color, even in the sunset wash. The birds are flitting from tree to tree, settling in for the night, chatting from nest to nest about the day.

"What?" Taren whispers.

"Pinch me," I say.

"What? No. Why?"

"Ouch," I say as Tisha pinches the skin of my hand. "I'm awake," I murmur.

"Yeah, so?" says Taren.

"This day feels dreamy. Or like my imagination has, for once, allowed me to think good things. To experience . . ." I search for the word that's exactly right. "Joy."

If there is ever to be a wall of memories in my house, I would want this moment to be at its heart.

We make a spectacle walking to Mr. Kingsley Pfupajena's house, decked out in Chedu's fashions.

"We haven't come this far to live on mute," Gogo Tapera says. "There is life and there is living; we're living."

Mr. Kingsley Pfupajena welcomes us as if he hadn't seen us a couple of hours ago. He's set up a photo area in the corner of his living room and made it fancy with a velvet maroon backdrop and colorful flowers and leaves—and he's placed a throne-ish chair in the middle. There's a camera on a tripod in front of the setting.

"Wait for me to place you," he says. "Miss Chianti Minana, you sit on the throne, here in the center. But look at you! Is this beauty or what?"

He gives me a beaming smile and sits me firmly down in the chair. He then takes ages arranging and rearranging everyone around me until the gogos complain about waiting so long for their drinks. In the end there's a revolt and Mr. Kingsley Pfupajena has to take the first few shots with Ambuya and the gogos in the first stages of their inevitable whisky party.

Baba is dressed completely differently, in new colors he's acquired from Mr. Kingsley Pfupajena's wardrobe, and it seems to have even changed his personality—or maybe he and our host had a whisky party of their own—because he's unusually animated and lit up.

"Look, Kiki, look!" he says, sweeping his arm out. "See what I did!" He beams at me, beckoning.

I step out onto the verandah and it takes my breath away. He really did do an outstanding job! The table is set for the most luxurious feast, with beautiful patterned plates on a deep-colored table cloth, flowers and greenery, wine goblets, candles, twinkling fairy lights, Christmas tinsel—which makes me laugh—and Christmas crackers, making me clap my hands for joy. More joy! I love Christmas crackers.

I don't stop to think about it; I give Baba a hug. "It's the best thing in the world," I say to him. "Thank you." This is not just trying, this is doing.

Baba holds me at arm's length, his hands on my shoulders. His smile pulls at a string and untangles the knot in my stomach.

"Chianti," he says, "I don't blame you for anything. It wasn't right that we deserted you."

The thing that has sat in my heart since that turn of midnight comes out. "You didn't answer my text. You were typing and stopped. Why?"

Baba hangs his head. "I was not in a good state of mind. I wanted to wait so you could see for yourself that no matter what was running through my mind or how I felt, one thing for sure is that I am your father. If you end up with two fathers, fine, but I am one of them."

Tears gather in my eyes, but my smile is the sun shining from inside me.

Gogo Tapera puts on the song "Dangerous" by Jah Prayzah, and Taren and Tisha start dancing—it's one of their favorites. Everyone cheers and Mama pulls me over to dance. I'm not as good at freestyle, but I'm happy, and if ever there was an occasion to dance, this is it.

When all the gogos join in, the party really gets going. We just about die of laughter when Tisha announces, "Gogo Stella, when I grow up I want to have a bum like yours so I can throw it about when I'm dancing."

Mama says, "Tisha, that's rude! Gogo is not one of your little friends!" But she laughs too.

"I'm just saying it's nice and fun to have," Tisha says.

"It's true!" Gogo Stella replies, tears of laughter in her eyes. "Tisha knows a good thing when she sees it."

I have to keep telling myself that I'm in real time, that it's not a dream. Even Baba is laughing and full of jokes. He and Mr. Kinsgley Pfupajena have cooked a feast: prawns, chicken, stewed roadrunner, deep-fried wings, a pork roast, brown peanut butter rice—my favorite—with fried greens, salad, stir-fried beef, the brown sadza from millet that Ambuya and the gogos love, roast potatoes, and for dessert, a trifle, ice cream, and more birthday cake.

At the table Mama sits next to me, with Taren on her other side. Everyone is talking and laughing. When Mama pulls me into a hug I don't resist, but I can't let myself open up yet. It's still not safe.

When "all are full and fed up" as Gogo Stella proclaims, we move to the sitting room and Mama takes out her guitar.

"Sing with me, Kiki," she says and begins to play the chords to a song she taught me—a song we always sing when we're having a good family day. It's about being happy because you can be. At first I don't want to do it, but I see how much everyone has done to make my birthday special and I understand it's not just others who have to put love into action, but also myself.

I go stand by Mama and make room in my heart for a song.

Mama and Baba volunteer to clean up. Tisha, Taren, and I are sitting on the cushy sofa with our sandals off. Taren leans over and opens a photo album that's on the coffee table next to her.

"Oh my gosh, look at you guys!" she says, leaning closer to examine the photos. "You were so young."

"We are still young, my dear," Gogo Tapera calls out from across the room.

"Sure, Gogo," Taren says. "Age is just a number, who cares?" With a gleam in her eyes she says, "So, I can smoke and drink whisky, right?"

"Wrong," Ambuya says.

"Wow, check this one." Taren slips a photo from its sleeve and holds it up. I know the photo when I see the date written neatly on the flip side. I've seen a copy in the box of memories.

"Oh yes," Gogo Stella says, "that was just before Independence Day. First chance to dress as adults. We'd gone to war as children and come out the other side fully grown."

As if an amplifier has been flipped on, the clatter of dishes in the kitchen becomes too loud, and there's a ringing in my ears as a question mark swings out of nowhere and lands with a thump in my chest.

"Let me see." I take the photo from Taren. It's Ambuya and Gogo Stella wearing full-sleeved dresses with pleated skirts, stockings, wide-brimmed hats, and tennis shoes.

"We got those clothes from a European organization that was giving assistance to women fighters from the front lines. They sent care packages. I guess that's where the idea for Chedu was formed—remember, Precious? We talked about how it would be wonderful to always dress so fine."

"Yes," Ambuya says, tilting her head in query as my eyes bore into hers. "What?" she says to me.

"Nothing . . . I just had a wild thought."

I shake my head, but I don't miss the silent exchange that passes between Ambuya and gogos Stella and Tapera. I doubt I'm going to sleep tonight.

TWENTY-TWO

I sneak out in the morning and make my way to Gogo Tapera's house. It was a late night, but they'll be up. Nothing keeps those ladies in bed after six. I barely slept, my mind whirling round and round. Long after Tisha and Taren were asleep, I pulled out the leatherbound notebook.

In a flash of clarity, I remember the day I discovered it—when I went to Gogo Ropa's and ended up in hospital. I'd had an impulse about the box file in the storage room. I'd snuck the notebook to my room and skimmed through it—torn pages, random dates, coordinates, names, and coded stories. The entry on the last page stayed in my mind. I thought about it for a while, then decided to go over to Gogo Ropa's in the hope she would tell me something useful.

Because of what happened that day, I stashed the story away and hadn't think about it again. Until last night, when I pored over the photos and the writing in the leatherbound notebook and sifted through my notes. It struck me like

Mr. Kingsley Pfupajena's club, appearing as if from thin air to administer a short sharp shock on the noggin.

They're waiting for me. All three of them. Sitting at Gogo Tapera's kitchen table with a steaming teapot and plates of vetkoeks.

We do our good mornings and I sit down.

"Tea?" Ambuya pours milky redbush into a cup.

I put the leatherbound notebook on the table.

"I haven't seen this for so many years," says Gogo Stella, picking it up.

"I thought I'd hidden it well enough," Gogo Tapera says, "but as a precaution I removed the more dangerous accounts."

"Why did we even keep it?' Gogo Stella asks.

Ambuya shrugs. "Just in case."

"Does Mama know?" I ask. I don't ask if it's true.

"She may, she may not. We've never talked about it," Ambuya says.

"But why?" I ask.

"There was no reason to."

The other gogos hum their agreement.

"But didn't Mama ever ask about her father?"

"He died in the war." They speak as a chorus.

"What about his family? Mama's paternal aunts and uncles, grandparents?"

"What about them?"

"Didn't she never ask about them?"

"We've never met them," Ambuya says.

"Yes, but . . ."

Gogo Tapera says, "It's only because you're now sixteen and you figured it out, but some things are better left alone."

"As I'm sure you can appreciate," Ambuya emphasizes.

"Okay, but how come I have the same birthmark as you?" I ask her.

"Not surprising. We are blood, after all."

True enough, I guess.

There is silence. We reach for our tea as if synchronized. I slide the notebook toward me and open it at the last page. I read the neat writing again.

15 November 1979, Arusha

I have named her after the Fox who will carry her to the Songbirds of the Savanna. The Leopard changed his spots and even now the Hawk is circling. All is lost. A Ghost cannot be caught until it shows itself. Long live the Ghost. We shall meet again after freedom. Viva.

The rest of it is blurred by water stains.

"It was the dates. In that photo with Gogo Stella," I say to Ambuya, "you should've been about to give birth to Mama, but you weren't pregnant. It didn't make sense. I checked in other photos—nothing. And then there you were with Mama."

I wait for denials. There are none.

"I had a niggling in my mind that wouldn't stop. You wouldn't talk about Sekuru, so I was searching for clues when I came across this notebook. I recognized Gogo

Ropa's writing. She's the Ghost, isn't she? She told me they sang a song about her—Hokoyo Chipokouyo, beware the ghost. I googled Mama's name to see if it had a meaning in an African language. It means 'we are finished' to the Tumbuka people, who live in Tanzania, as well as Malawi and Zambia. 'We are finished' is also what *Tapera* means in Shona."

The faces around me are blank. They simply sip their teas and nibble on their vetkoeks.

"So Mama was born in Tanzania. Gogo Ropa named Mama after Gogo Tapera. Gogo Tapera, you brought Mama back from Tanzania and gave her to the Songbirds of the Savanna—Ambuya and Gogo Stella. And Ambuya, being older than Gogo Stella by a year, you got dibs on the kid."

Ambuya simply raises an eyebrow and continues to drink her tea.

"I don't know who the Leopard or the Hawk are, but since both are predatory creatures I think it was a bad scene and Gogo Ropa had to disappear."

No one says anything.

"It was a harrowing few years," Gogo Tapera says finally. "People didn't ask questions. We returned from war and Precious had a baby."

"And Gogo Ropa? Where did she go? Didn't she want Mama?"

It's Ambuya who speaks. "She turned up here in 1983. We were still in the old house—the one she lives in now. She didn't remember having had a baby. She didn't talk much. She needed a lot of care. She stayed more in the rural areas with what was left of our family. None of us know what happened when she went into hiding. We let her be. We've all got things we don't want to remember."

"And Mama's father?" I will probably never get this level of cooperation again.

"He died in the war!" they say emphatically.

"There is nothing to be gained by turning over stones that have remained in place for so many years," Gogo Tapera says. "Leave it be now, all of it. Leave it be."

"Secrets always come out," I say.

"It's not a secret," Gogo Stella replies. "We just don't talk about it. The trouble with calling it a secret is that the nature of it changes, and it becomes a disagreeable thing to keep. But if everyone knows, and no one talks about it . . ." Her pause is loaded. ". . . then it's just another thing we choose to archive."

"You have enough wisdom at this point in your life to understand the power of words," Ambuya says. "This is not a mystery that needs solving. It's just family."

I want to say that it's important to know things, to have history. But I know, too, that sometimes it's better to let a sleeping dog dream in peace. Life's still going to be there when it wakes up.

TWENTY-THREE

No one has noticed that I left the house early. I simply walk in with Ambuya, the gogos, and Mr. Kingsley Pfupajena for breakfast. Tisha and Taren haven't got up yet. Mama suspects, I can tell, but she lets it go.

I'm trying not to watch her for signs that she knows Ambuya is not her birth mother. What I now understand is that families are complicated. This whole family of mine, even before Ambuya, is a thing with its own form. I guess that's why they call them family trees. There's no consistency of structure—no two branches are the same.

As we're cleaning up the kitchen after brunch, I think about the fact that Ambuya is not my direct grandmother and that it doesn't make a difference in how I feel. She is Ambuya to me, as she has always been, and it's heartwarming that genetics made me take after her, even down to the birthmark. It wouldn't make any difference to Tisha and Taren either, and all at once I understand it makes no difference to them that I have a different biological dad. I'm glad I got to learn about Gogo Ropa through the letters and pages she wrote, and from the moments she's been present.

"What are you thinking about so deeply?" Taren nudges me, and I realize I've been holding the broom and staring into my thoughts.

"Nothing," I say. "It was fun last night."

"Best birthday ever," Tisha pipes up. "Even if it wasn't mine, I still enjoyed it one hundred percent."

"Me too," Taren laughs. "I'm almost glad the brouhaha happened."

Mama and Baba aren't exactly back together, but they're acting more couply. It seems they're going to fake it till they make it. Maybe we should never leave, because without the safety net of the grannies they won't have to be on their best behavior.

Mama calls me to the verandah, where she's sitting with a book. My early morning visit with the gogos feels like a trip to a different country, in a life that belongs to another me, way before now.

"Come and sit with me," Mama says, indicating the space next to her on the sofa. I take the seat across from her. She sighs. "Chianti."

"Why did you give me that name, anyway?"

Mama leans forward. "One summer, Mama's expat friends invited us to visit them in Tuscany. I was seventeen and we weren't agreeing on much, but while we were there, you couldn't be unhappy if you tried. It was beautiful and bright. It was a real vacation, not just me tagging along while Mama worked. We ate and explored and laughed the way we used to. We were in the Chianti region. And that's what was in my mind when you were born. I thought that's what your life would be like: bright, beautiful . . . happy."

I hadn't expected that, so all I say is, "Oh."

"Yes," Mama says, "I bet you thought it was because I love alcohol." She laughs shortly. "I don't blame you, I guess. As role models go, I probably could do better."

I don't think she's a bad mother or a bad person, but I don't want to commit to forgiveness yet.

"About your biological father . . ." she starts.

"Was it him that day at the doctor's?"

Surprised, Mama pauses and rearranges what she had prepared to say. "You remember that? Wow! It was the ER, you were running a temperature. He was with his wife—she had a broken arm." Mama makes a strange face.

"What was he saying to you?"

She laughs sadly. "He thought I was following him." She shakes her head, and a parade of emotions take turns on her face. "I didn't tell him about you. He believes you're Tinashe's." She shrugs. "He might suspect but he's too busy with himself."

"Would he want me to live with him if he knew about me?" My heart is tumbling about—I couldn't imagine such a thing.

"I wouldn't let that happen, unless . . . unless you'd want that." At this she looks pained, almost scared. "We've talked about it, your dad and I, and we don't think it's necessary to say anything, unless you want to meet him."

"No!" I don't even entertain it for a millisecond. "I've never wished for another dad." The thought of it is like someone strangling my heart.

"You should tell him that," Mama says. "He thinks he's boring and strict." She laughs, properly this time.

"Maybe at some point I'll change my mind about meeting my bio dad," I say, "but for now I'm good."

Mama shifts in her seat and worries the nail she's been picking. "There are cultural issues, bloodlines and stuff."

At this, my own blood comes rushing to my head. If your father's family consults their ancestors, they'll be informed that you're not where you're supposed to be, and it can cause problems in your life.

I hear Mama from far away. "Chianti . . ." She's by my chair, squeezing my hands hard.

"Ow!"

"Chianti, breathe."

"I'm breathing," I say, taking a gulp of air and letting it out slowly.

Mama gives me a little shake. "It's okay, Chianti, look at me."

I'm angry again and I try to get my hands back, but Mama doesn't let go.

"Chianti." Her voice is sharp and insisting, so I look. "I spoke to the gogos, your dad and I did."

"And?"

"And everyone agreed there's no need to cross bridges until we have to, but along the way we may come to them, okay? We have to be grown-up about this—talk about it and be in agreement about whatever we decide. Okay?"

"Okay," I mumble, "but this is really unfair."

Mama sighs and sits down in her spot. "It was never my intention to hurt you. Never ever. I love you with no reservations. I don't regret choosing Tinashe; I do regret the lie. I was afraid and then I was ashamed. When you were born I suffered postpartum depression. He was the one who took care of you. Ambuya too. She knew something was wrong. I picked a fight with her and kept it going all these years. I knew I would eventually tell her, and I thought she might make me tell your dad. It got worse over the years, the guilt. The longer I left it, the harder it became to say anything and the more I despised myself. I shouldn't have let you find out the way you did. And I shouldn't have left you and gone on tour afterward. I was in a daze. I couldn't believe what I'd done, I didn't want to think of it. I brought us so low."

I don't say anything. People make mistakes, and I'm not angry anymore. I'm scared and I hate how it feels. I want to sit in the dimly lit living room and listen to Gogo Ropa talking about the war. About running away from home to other lives. About love being an action. It hits me that Mama never knew her own father either.

I curl my legs up under me and turn my attention to the garden. The chirping of the birds brings me to the present, the light breeze cools my neck. Birds are lucky—they just fly from place to place, they don't care about ancestors or bloodlines. They hatch their young, feed them, then kick them out to get on with it.

I'm not aware I've broken the silence with my sigh, until Mama speaks.

"Funny thing is you're a lot like your dad—Tinashe. Responsible, kind, levelheaded, but no pushover. And you're creative, like me. We couldn't have made a better kid."

It's not the nice things she's saying that releases the tight fist in my chest. It's the fact that for the first time Mama hears not only the echo of her own voice, but the sound of mine.

TWENTY-FOUR

I lie awake, listening to the birds outside our bedroom window, watching the light filter through the curtains. These last few days I've been so alert that when the sun comes round it already feels late. I no longer have the tiredness that had gotten hold of me when I first arrived. My brain won't stop working; even in my sleep it's busy with dreams. I'm dying to get up and talk to Ambuya.

Taren catches me before I leave, and together we sneak out to Gogo Tapera's house. I give Taren the quick notes of the situation on the way.

"Gogo Ropa is not well. She's had to go to a place in the mountains, in Vumba, to recover, and I want to work on a surprise for when she comes home."

"I don't really know her," Taren says. "But if she's Ambuya's sister, then she's our grandmother too."

"Yes," I say.

Taren doesn't ask any more questions. A part of her is

still asleep. In the early morning, you can convince Taren of anything.

Ambuya opens up Gogo Ropa's house for us and together we bring in the supplies I need. I kick off my project in the room next to the one with Gogo Ropa's wall of sorrow. I'm happy that Ambuya locked that door, so none of us have to go in there and be a part of the sadness inside.

When I explain my plan, Mr. Kingsley Pfupajena volunteers to buy extra paints and brushes. I write him a list.

"You're a thoughtful young woman, God bless you," he says.

"I'm going to draw the most important things in the middle of the wall," I tell Taren. "You and Tisha are going to make the leaves, flowers, and birds while I finish here."

In the middle of the wall I draw Ambuya, the gogos, and Mr. Kingsley Pfupajena. I put Baba, myself, and Tisha on one side and on the other, Mama and Taren. Everyone is wearing their clothes from last night, and for Gogo Ropa, I draw what I imagine she might've worn, complete with bright eyeshadow. Drawing is easy; painting is the hard part.

We work until lunch when Ambuya, the gogos, and Mr. Kingsley Pfupajena come in to check our progress.

"Wow!" Ambuya exclaims. "This is beautiful, girls."

I've painted everyone's clothes, but doing faces is harder and needs more concentration, so I'll leave that for last. Taren and Tisha have finished making and cutting out the flowers, leaves, and birds, and after painting the background green, they'll stick them on the wall. We stop to assess. It really is amazing. I can't wait until it's finished.

Ambuya makes us stop for lunch, and we troop down to Mr. Kingsley Pfupajena's. It's simple beef and chicken barbequed outside on his grill, with sadza, fried cabbage, and a chakalaka sauce. Mama and Baba stay behind to clean up again—at least they're good for something!

On impulse I go get the shoeboxes I decorated and, back at Gogo Ropa's house, I place them one on top of the other in a corner. A small memento of where I began with my family collages. I'm going to paint over the prison bars on Mama's box so she's surrounded by blue sky and clouds.

In the end, everyone helps. They cover the wall with Taren and Tisha's cut-outs while I paint the faces. We work until midnight and when we finish we step back and take stock.

It's not perfect, but it's beautiful—all of us standing in our best clothes, a blue sky above and around us, flowering trees full of colorful birds. I've amended my birthday outfit by adding a red heart on my chest and glitter to make it stand out.

"Chianti," Mama says, "this is special. Thank you." There are tears in her eyes. Baba puts an arm around Mama and hugs me against him with his other arm.

After cleaning up our paints and sweeping the floor, we move a single bed into a corner of the room. Ambuya and the gogos have spent the day making cheerful covers and pillows and sheer curtains to let in light. Mr. Kingsley Pfupajena promises to paint the other walls a warm yellow in the next couple of days. There's no whisky party. We go straight to bed. I feel good.

When Gogo Ropa comes home, she won't have to sleep in the room with the wall of sorrow. If she wants to, she can be in here with the mural so she's not alone. She can be surrounded by nature—the trees, leaves, birds, and flowers are for her to enjoy. She can sit and remember why she went to war and that we, her family, are living the life she wanted for us. That we are, in many ways, free.

EPILOGUE

Ambuya creeps into our room early on our last morning, asking if we want to go to the market. All of us say yes. Tisha and Taren are excited because they've never been.

"Sssh." Ambuya puts a finger to her lips. "Don't wake your mother."

"Why?" Tisha whispers.

"She hates the market, but she always wants to come. It's a pain for everyone to hear her complaints."

"I heard that and I'm coming." Mama's voice from behind makes us jump.

Ambuya rolls her eyes and mutters, "I should've sent a text . . . Okay, let's go. But Tamara, one grumble or suggestion of how the place could be improved and you're walking home."

In the end, even Baba and Mr. Kingsley Pfupajena come. We go in two cars and split up when we arrive. I go with Ambuya and Tisha, and Taren goes with Gogo Stella and Gogo Tapera. Mama and Baba go together.

Winston is beaming. "Gogaz!" he greets Ambuya. "How are you? The shipment came in, but you would never believe the news about town—haaa, it's astonishing . . ."

Ambuya should win an award for acting. With every sentence in Winston's account of what happened to the robbers, she's more astonished, saying, "Don't tell me!"

"Gogaz, the forest is no place for nefarious deeds. Sooner or later, if you are doing wrong to others, it will catch up with you. We're just trying to eat—we've never stolen or done harm."

"Sure, sure, Winston, this is true," Ambuya agrees. "What an incredible story. But I've seen many inexplicable things in my life, so I am not surprised."

"And what's more amazing is I heard Sanderson Kwete, the bartender at Sanganai Pub, had a dream that foretold catastrophe in the forest—a pride of lions roaring at the mouth of the cave that no one enters. Yes, that should've been warning enough. People don't take such things seriously until they see it for themselves."

"So what happened to the smugglers?" Ambuya asks.

Winston scratches his head. "Nothing. The robbers had tied them up and left them behind. They fell asleep hoping to be rescued in the morning and when they woke up, they were free."

"Fell asleep?" Ambuya asks. "Just there in the forest?"

"What else were they going to do, Gogaz? At least they avoided the beating they got from the robbers last time."

"So they won't be afraid to continue running supplies?"

"I think it will be fine. The robbers most likely won't bother them again."

Ambuya smiles, and Winston's eyes turn shrewd.

"You advanced funds for this bale." He lowers his voice. "Could you have had anything to do with the goings-on in the bush?"

Ambuya laughs. "Winston! Am I not a living, breathing woman of a sophisticated age?"

"Sure, Gogaz," he replies. "But you are also cunning and unpredictable women."

"And don't forget it," Ambuya says, ending that line of communication.

Winston gets the message. "Yah," he says, as if the last couple of minutes never happened. "It will be better soon, I'm sure. Any day now the ban will be lifted and things will return to normal."

Ambuya laughs. "What is normal, Winston?"

"The settings we know, Gogaz, the settings we know."

"That's all a body can ask for, I suppose. Now, let's see what you have for us."

In the car we laugh and laugh. The vendors all had different variations of the story—some said there was a ghost, others said there were drums, another said one of the robbers heard his dead grandfather calling him from beyond.

Shame; sorry for Mama and Baba in their car talking normal stories, while we're having such fun reliving our adventure.

Mama was lucky to have Ambuya and her sisters as her mothers, and we are lucky to have them as our grandmothers. The rest of it doesn't matter.

My family is different from other families. There's no guarantee things will be better immediately, but for now I don't care. I am happy, and it feels like home.

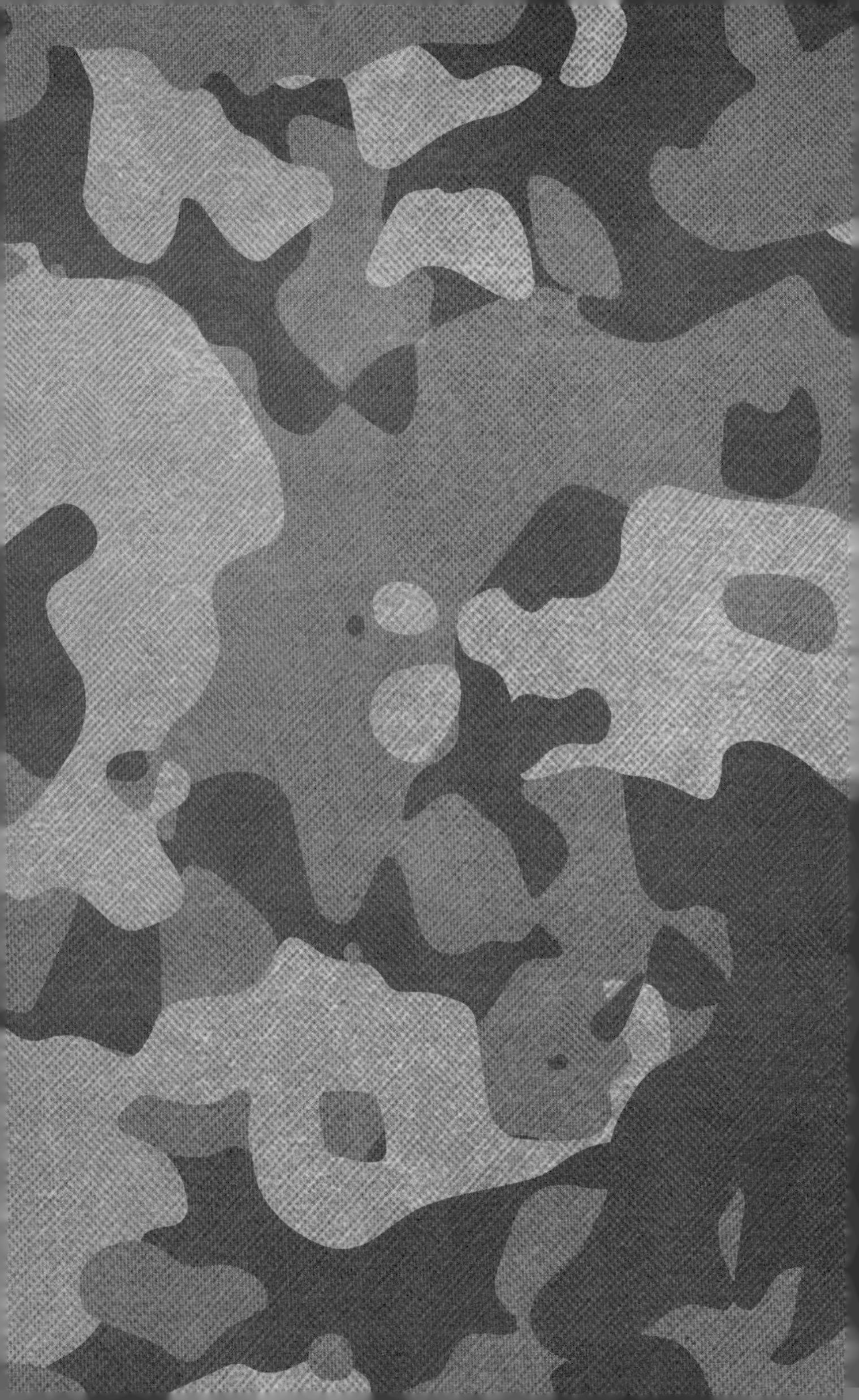

Questions for Discussion

1. In what ways does the revelation that Baba is not Chianti's biological father immediately impact the family?
2. Compare Ambuya, the gogos, and Mr. Kingsley Pfupajena with elders you know or with other characters in this age range from different stories. What similarities do you find? What makes these characters distinctive or unusual?
3. Why is Chianti drawn to the "puzzle pieces" of the gogos' past?
4. The elders share several pithy insights with Chianti. Which one did you find most moving or thought-provoking?
5. Pick one of Chianti's reflections on war that stuck with you. How might it apply to other difficult experiences?

6. Why doesn't Chianti want to speak to her sisters? What does she fear? What assumptions does she make?
7. Which family secret most surprised you when it was revealed, and why?
8. According to Ambuya, what is the difference between a secret and "just another thing we choose to archive"? Do you agree? Why or why not?
9. How does Chianti's mural in Gogo Ropa's house synthesize what she's experienced and learned during her stay with Ambuya?
10. How does Chianti's relationship with each parent shift between the beginning and the end of the story? What do you predict for the family's future?

Glossary

ambuya: a Shona word meaning "grandmother"; can also be used for a respected elder

batman: a personal attendant to a military officer, often assigned to perform chores, run errands, and deliver messages

boubou: a long, flowing robe commonly worn in West African nations

chakalaka: a vegetable relish originating in South Africa

Chimoio: a city in Mozambique

chimurenga: a Shona word meaning "revolutionary struggle"; the Zimbabwe War of Independence (1964–1979), in which the Zimbabwe African National Liberation Army (ZANLA) fought against the Rhodesian Army, is often called the Second Chimurenga

chipoko: a Shona word for the spirit or soul of a dead person

Christmas cracker: a decorative, brightly wrapped cardboard tube that makes a snapping noise when pulled apart; traditionally used at Christmas in the United Kingdom and its current and former colonies, including Zimbabwe, a former Commonwealth nation

gogo: a colloquial term meaning "grandmother" in the Shona language; used to address an elder

Gudo: a baboon character who is routinely outwitted by the wily Tsuro in Shona folklore

Harare: the capital and largest city of Zimbabwe

Mozambique: a country in Southeast Africa, east of Zimbabwe

msasa: a type of tree that grows in southern and eastern Africa

muzukuru: a Shona word meaning "grandchild"

Mutare: a large city in eastern Zimbabwe

Nyadzonya Raid: also known as Operation Eland, a 1976 attack by the Rhodesian Army on a ZANLA training and refugee camp that killed more than a thousand people

pungwe: a Shona word that literally means "sunrise," commonly used to refer to a nighttime vigil, including gatherings held by the Zimbabwe African National Liberation Army during the War of Independence

sadza: cornmeal or cornmeal-based porridge

salaula: a Zambian term literally meaning "to select from a pile," used to refer to secondhand clothing markets in many African nations

sekuru: a Shona word meaning "grandfather"; can also be used for a respected elder

Shona: an ethnic group native to southern Africa and one of the sixteen official languages of Zimbabwe, also spoken in Mozambique and parts of southern Africa

Tanzania: a country in East Africa, north of Mozambique

Tsuro: a trickster hare who outsmarts larger animals in Shona folklore

vetkoek: fried dough bread originating in South Africa

Vumba: a mountainous region along the Zimbabwe-Mozambique border

Zimbabwe: a country in southeast Africa, bordered by Mozambique to the east, South Africa to the south, Botswana to the southwest, and Zambia to the north

Acknowledgments

Many thanks to Sarah Odedina (Accord Literary) and Julia Churchill (A. M. Heath) for happy Mondays. Thanks to Lauren Atherton, who loved the gogos so much and worked so hard to whip the story into its best shape. Thank you to everyone at Zephyr and at Lerner/Carolrhoda, including Amy Fitzgerald for such dedication to detail.

About the Author

Blessing Musariri is an award-winning author of short stories, children's books, radio and screenplays, and contemporary adult fiction. Blessing lives in Harare, Zimbabwe.

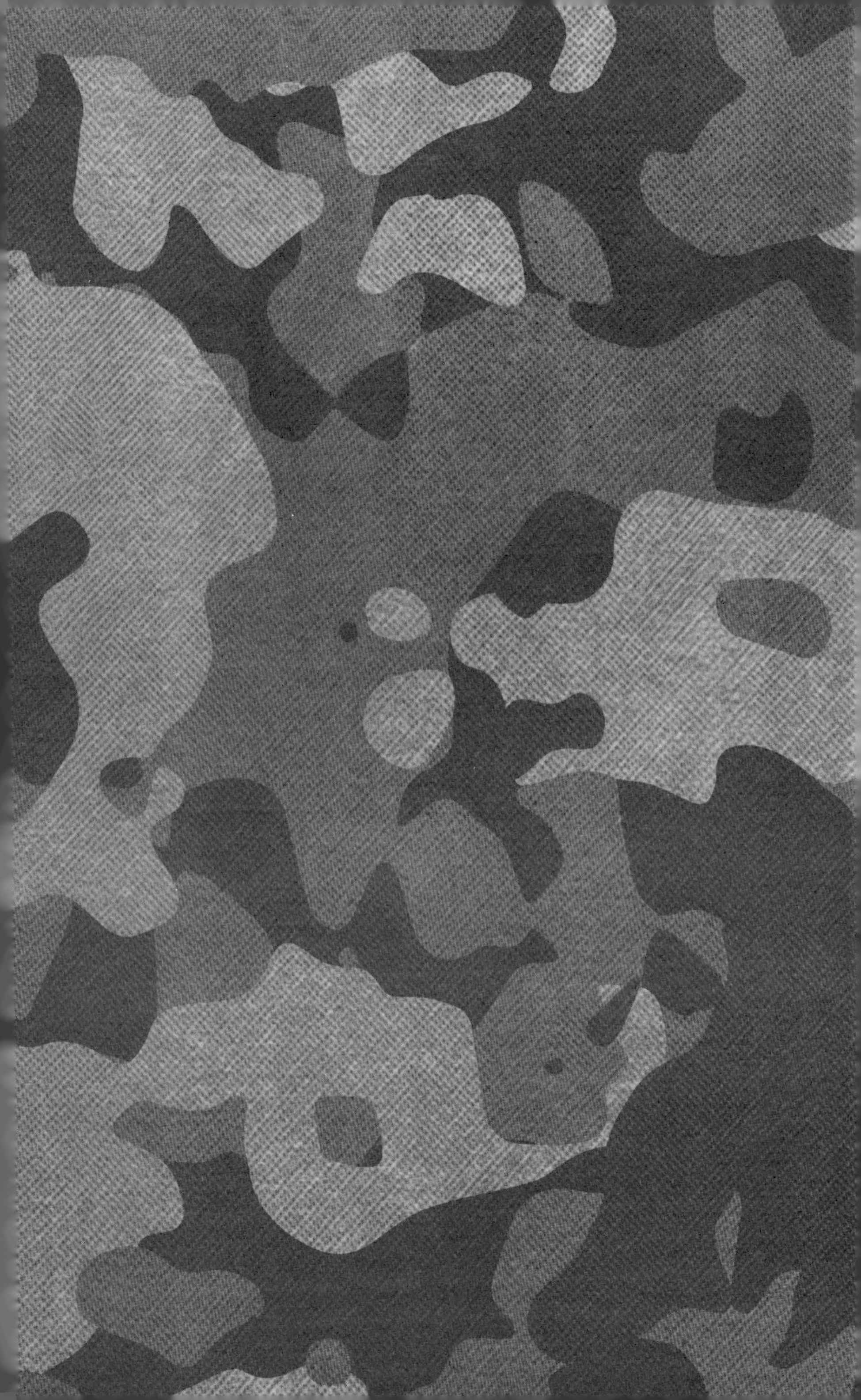